The Trailsman:

COLORADO
DIAMOND DUPE

Jon Sharpe

The Trailsman:

COLORADO
DIAMOND DUPE

WHEELER PUBLISHING, INC.
ROCKLAND, MA

★ AN AMERICAN COMPANY ★

T.F.

Published in Large Print by arrangement with Signet, an imprint of
New American Library, a division of Penguin Putnam, Inc. in the United
States and Canada

Wheeler Large Print Book Series.

Set in 16 pt Plantin.

Library of Congress Cataloging-in-Publication Data

Sharpe, Jon
    The trailsman: Colorado diamond dupe / Jon Sharpe.
        p. (large print) cm.(Wheeler large print book series)
    ISBN 1-56895-888-9 (softcover)
    1. Large type books. I. Title. II. Series

813'.54—dc21   00-039863
                                                              CIP

The Trailsman

Beginnings...they bend the tree and they mark the man. Skye Fargo was born when he was eighteen. Terror was his midwife, vengeance his first cry. Killing spawned Skye Fargo, ruthless, cold-blooded murder. Out of the acrid smoke of gunpowder still hanging in the air, he rose, cried out a promise never forgotten.

The Trailsman they began to call him all across the west: searcher, scout, hunter, the man who could see where others only looked, his skills for hire but not his soul, the man who lived each day to the fullest, yet trailed each tomorrow. Skye Fargo, the Trailsman, the seeker who could take the wildness of a land and the wanting of a woman and make them his own.

Colorado, 1860—where the allure of a woman's eyes can be as sparkling as the glint of precious gems and every bit as dangerous as the dark chasm of an open mineshaft...

1

The high-pitched cry of a woman in pain brought the big man in buckskins to a halt. His piercing lake blue eyes scanned the opposite side of the busy street and spied a small crowd in front of a millinery, a store devoted to ladies' headwear. Curiosity compelled him to see what was going on. Always cautious, he glanced both ways first. Denver's carriage drivers and wagoners were notorious for not caring who or what they ran over. Every month over a dozen dogs and cats and other stray animals were crushed under merciless grinding wheels, to say nothing of the occasional hapless humans.

Skye Fargo didn't intend to be one of them. But just as he strode off the boardwalk a speeding freight wagon careened around an intersection and bore down on him with all the abandon of stampeding buffalo.

The grizzled driver, cracking his whip, bawled like a drunk on a binge, "Out of my way, you clod!"

Skye Fargo couldn't rightly say what made him do what he did next. Ordinarily, he would have bounded to safety and let the wagon go on by. But not this particular morning. Maybe it was the headache he had from too much whiskey the night before. Maybe it was his irritable mood at having lost almost every last cent he had at poker. Or maybe it was simple resentment. Whatever the case, his Colt materialized in his hand, trained on the onrushing driver.

The man was no fool. He hauled on the reins for all he was worth, straining backward, throwing his entire weight into it as he shouted, "Whoa, there! Whoa! Whoa! Whoa!" The big wagon ground to a lurching halt, the lead animals snorting and stomping two yards from where Fargo stood.

Fargo slowly lowered the Colt, then twirled it into his holster.

"What the hell is the matter with you, mister?" the driver hollered. "Are you lookin' to get yourself killed? Learn how to cross a street, why don't you?"

"Learn how to drive," Fargo retorted. He was strongly tempted to haul the cantankerous cuss from the driver's box but another cry drew his eyes to the fringes of the crowd. Taller than most, Fargo could see over the onlookers to the center of the commotion. And he didn't like what he saw.

Sprawled on his rump in front of a store was a portly gentleman in a white suit and matching bowler. His ruddy cheeks were puffed out in rage, his thick lips twitching like those of a wild boar about to bite. "I demand that you unhand her this instant, sir!" he fumed.

The object of his wrath was a ruffian in rumpled clothes and a floppy hat. The man, grinning lecherously, had hold of a young woman's wrists. "Settle down, missy," he sternly advised. "This doesn't involve you."

"It does so!" the woman responded. "He's my father! You had no right to knock him down!"

"If he doesn't want his head bashed in, he shouldn't go around bumping into folks." The man gave her left wrist a sharp twist and she cried out again. "Now behave yourself, or I'm liable to really get rough."

The young woman did no such thing. She was in her early twenties, a stunning beauty whose golden hair spilled over her slender shoulders in curly waves. A green dress clung to her luscious form like a second skin, accenting the ample sweep of her bosom and her flat stomach. When she moved, the dress clung to her legs, highlighting the splendid contours of her shapely thighs. Her blue eyes flashed like lightning as she drew back a foot to kick her tormentor. "Let go of me!"

Laughing, the ruffian sidestepped her kick, then pushed her against the wall. "You take after your pa, don't you, girl? Neither of you know how to listen worth a damn."

There were upward of twenty onlookers but not a single one was disposed to lend the young woman a hand. Her tormentor's size probably had something to do with it. He was a big man, nearly as big as Fargo, only grimier and scruffier. In addition, a Remington rested on the man's right hip, and he had the air of someone who wouldn't hesitate to use it if provoked.

"Leave her be!" the woman's portly father railed. Propping his pudgy hands under him, he sought to rise.

"Stay where you are, chubby," the bully snapped, planting the sole of his right boot in the father's chest, knocking him to the ground. "I'll get to you in a moment."

3

Fargo had seen enough. He barreled through the crowd, drawing frowns of disapproval and a few oaths. When he reached the man holding the blonde, he didn't politely ask for the ruffian to release her. He didn't tap the man on the shoulder, or clear his throat to get the man's attention. Fargo simply jerked his Colt, spun the hardcase around, and brought the barrel crashing down onto the crown of the man's brown hat with enough force to bring a bull moose to its knees. The man crumpled, oozing like melted wax into a disjointed heap.

Replacing the Colt for the second time in as many minutes, Fargo touched his hat brim to the astounded blonde. "He won't bother you any more ma'am."

"Thank you, kind sir," she responded. Clasping his right hand in both her warm palms, she gently squeezed. "This uncouth lout was going to kick my father's teeth in. All because my father bumped into him coming out of the store."

Fargo pegged her accent as from somewhere in the deep South. Georgia, perhaps, or Alabama. "Denver isn't Savannah. This is the frontier. Men out here are rougher than those you're used to." As she withdrew her hands, one of her fingernails lightly scraped the side of his forefinger.

"So we're finding out," the blonde said, and smiled, showing pearly, even teeth. "Goodness gracious. Where are my manners? I haven't properly introduced myself. Delicia Cadwell is my name, and I'm right pleased

4

to make your acquaintance." She bent her knee in a playful curtsy.

"Delicia," Fargo said, rolling the name on the tip of his tongue as he would a piece of hard candy. It fit her as nicely as her dress. She was a genuine beauty, her dazzling eyes and cherry lips enough to make a man's head spin. The tantalizing fragrance of lilacs tingled his nose as he introduced himself.

Her father snorted. "Harrumph! I don't suppose either of you would care to assist me to my feet? The social amenities can wait until my dignity is restored."

Fargo gripped the man's elbow and boosted him upright. Now that the hardcase had been dealt with, the crowd was dispersing, with everyone venturing on about their business.

"Allow me to add my gratitude to my daughter's. Rupert T. Cadwell, at your service." The father shook Fargo's hand with sweaty fingers as fat as sausages. "I can't thank you enough, Mr. Fargo. Not that your help was truly needed, however. Another moment, and I'd have risen up and given that cretin a clout that would have left him senseless for a week."

Given how weakly Cadwell shook his hand, Fargo doubted the man could hit anyone hard enough to give them more than a mild bruise. "Glad I could be of help." Prying his fingers loose, he nodded at Delicia. "Take care."

"What's your hurry to rush off?" she asked.

"Indeed," Rupert echoed. "We would be honored if you would permit us to show our appreciation in more tangible ways. How

5

about twenty dollars?" he said, reaching under his white jacket.

"There's no need," Fargo declined. He needed a good, stiff drink more than money right now. Just one, to ease the dull ache in his head.

Delicia grabbed his arm. "Please let us do something. How about if we treat you to a meal? Or at least a piece of pie? There's a quaint little restaurant just down the street."

Fargo hesitated. Six or seven cups of coffee would have the same effect as a glass of rotgut. And he had skipped breakfast to conserve his meager funds. Plus he still had his hotel bill to pay, as well as the stabling fee for the Ovaro. "Fact is, I haven't eaten yet."

"Then it's settled!" Rupert declared, adjusting his bowler as he led the way. "Despite what just occurred, I must say I've taken quite a liking to this city. It has a wild aspect I find rather invigorating."

"And dangerous," Fargo amended. But he agreed. He liked Denver, too. Started only a couple of years ago by rival factions, it was now being billed as the "gateway to the Rockies" and the "San Francisco of the foothills" by the *Rocky Mountain News,* the city's one and only newspaper.

Every time Fargo passed through the territory, Denver had grown larger. It now boasted fifteen hotels and boardinghouses, eleven restaurants, two schools, two theaters, about thirty retail establishments, and twenty-five bars and saloons. To say nothing of its bawdy houses. Fargo could remember when town lots went for twenty dollars each; now they were ten times as much.

"Danger is part and parcel of life, is it not?" Rupert said. "There is an element of risk in everything we do. Speaking for myself, I've learned to minimize the risks but accept them as inevitable." He gestured grandly. "Take my latest enterprise. I knew it would expose my daughters to some small degree of peril, but did I let that stop me? I certainly did not."

"Daughters?" Fargo said.

It was Delicia who answered. "My older sister, Amity, is off by herself. We'll rejoin her later at the Grand."

Fargo was impressed. The Grand Hotel was one of the best the city boasted, as elegant as any found in St. Louis or New Orleans, and ridiculously expensive. The Cadwells had to have money to spare to afford to stay there.

The restaurant they had picked bore a painted sign that proudly announced it was known as THE GRUB. Inside, most of the long tables were empty. It would be hours yet before hungry workers filed in for their midday meal. Out of habit Fargo chose a table in a far corner where he could sit with his back to the wall. He held out a chair for Delicia.

Rupert T. Cadwell sank into another with a sigh. "Quite frankly, Mr. Fargo, I'm glad you agreed. I needed to get off my feet. All morning my sweet Delicia has been dragging me from store to store so she could admire the latest dresses and bonnets. I'm worn to a frazzle."

Merry mirth tinkled from Delicia's smooth throat. "Oh, please, Father. You protest too much. What else did you have to do?"

"True," Rupert said. "Until Amity is done, our time is our own." He folded his hands on the table. "So tell me, Mr. Fargo. If it's not improper of me to inquire, exactly what do you do for a living?"

"From time to time I scout for the army. Or work as a guide. Among other things." Fargo didn't go into detail. His personal life was none of their business.

"Scout and guide, you say?" Rupert repeated, his forehead puckering. "Then it's safe to assume you're quite knowledgeable about the mountains. You must know them inside and out, as it were."

Fargo shrugged. "Better than most, I suppose." The truth was, his wanderlust had taken him from one end of the Rockies to the other, from Canada clear down to Mexico. Few frontiersmen knew the vast region west of the Mississippi River as well as he did.

"How fortuitous," Rupert remarked, swapping looks with his daughter. "Perhaps our meeting was preordained. In the next day or two we will be in need of someone with your expertise. How much do you charge to act as a guide?"

"It depends on where you want to go," Fargo said. Further talk was interrupted by the arrival of the waitress, a middle-aged woman in a homespun dress and long apron. Fargo ordered a double portion of eggs and bacon, a slab of ham, and two sides of toast.

He also told her to keep the coffee coming "until it comes out my ears."

Rupert chuckled while studying the menu. "You have quite an appetite. A trait I share." He pursed his lips, then tilted his plump face toward the waitress. "I'd like one of your apple pies, my dear—"

"A slice of apple pie," she said, scribbling on her pad.

"No, no. A *whole* pie," Rupert said. "Along with coffee and a heaping bowl of sugar." He winked good-naturedly. "Unsweetened coffee is an affront to my taste buds." As she departed he grinned at Delicia. "Did you see how she looked at me, daughter? I'd say she was smitten."

Delicia sighed. "Father, please. It's getting to the point where I can't take you out in public without a leash."

Fargo and Rupert laughed. Fargo found himself liking the pair, especially Delicia. When she leaned back, her breasts thrust against her dress as if striving to burst through the silken material. He couldn't help imaging how she would look unclothed and felt himself stir below the table. "What about you?" he asked her. "You didn't order anything."

"Unlike my father, I'm not a bottomless pit. Two meals a day are more than enough for me. Not six or seven."

"Now, now," Rupert rebutted. "Don't begrudge a man his minor pleasures. Eating to excess is one of my few vices. Would you rather I drank to excess?"

Delicia reached over to stroke her father's

ruddy cheek. "Stick to eating. I'd rather live with a whale than a drunk any day."

And so it went for the next hour, father and daughter bantering while Fargo listened and ate. The eggs were done to perfection, the bacon thick with fat and grease, the toast layered heavy with butter. He washed it all down with four cups of coffee, then sat back to enjoy a couple more.

Fargo learned the pair were from Atlanta, that they had arrived in Denver four days ago, and that they had been taking in the sights and doing what they kept referring to as "research." "You haven't said what you do for a living," Fargo commented at one point.

"How remiss of me," Rupert said. "Perhaps I should have given you my credentials when we first met." He produced a small card from his jacket pocket and handed it over with a flourish. Boldly imprinted upon it were the words, PROFESSOR RUPERT T. CADWELL, GEMOL-OGIST EXTRAORDINAIRE. D.G., P.O.R.M, M.S. Fargo had no idea what the initials meant, and said as much.

"They stand for the degrees I've earned. In short, it means I'm a qualified gemologist. One of the foremost in this country, perhaps the entire world. It's my passion in life to travel the globe in search of rare gems and minerals."

"Like gold and silver?" Fargo said, thinking of the hordes who had flooded into the region recently on the heels of a gold strike. Hundreds arrived every month, lured by the chance to get rich quick. Most were doomed to severe disappointment, for every fledgling prospector who struck it rich, thousands worked their fingers to the bone for naught.

"I'm more interested in rare gems," Rupert responded. "Rubies, emeralds, diamonds, and the like."

"Too bad no one has found any here," Fargo idly remarked. Swallowing some coffee, he saw the father and daughter exchange another peculiar glance. Both grinned, as if at a private joke.

"If they did, it would be the find of the century," Rupert said. "Yet the prospect is not all that farfetched. Many of the geologic conditions in other regions of the world that have spawned precious gems are also found in the Rockies."

"Father—" Delicia said rather harshly.

"Never fear, my dear, I won't give our little secret away," Rupert assured her. "Besides, nothing I could divulge would allow our newfound friend to get the jump on us. He lacks my vast knowledge, my years of experience, my unflagging dedication and tireless persistence."

"And your humility," Delicia quipped.

Chortling, Rupert slapped his thigh. "Did you hear her, Mr. Fargo? My own flesh and blood! I tell you, the young have no respect for their elders anymore. All they do is give a parent sass and grief."

Just then the door swung inward with a resounding crash. Into the restaurant stalked the ruffian Fargo had pistol-whipped, along with a pair of beefy friends. They surveyed the room, then made a beeline for their table, the

11

hardcase leading his grungy companions with his thumbs hooked boldly in his gunbelt.

The patrons gaped, unsure what to expect.

"Hold on, there," the waitress said, moving to intercept the trio. "What's the meaning of this?"

"Don't butt in, if you know what's good for you," the leader growled, and rudely shoved her out of the way. "The same holds for the rest of you!" he announced, glaring about the room. "Anyone who sticks their nose in will wish they hadn't."

No one spoke. No one moved.

Squaring his shoulders, the hardcase advanced to the table. "Didn't reckon on seeing me again, I bet."

Rupert was a living portrait of indignation. "What do you want? Why do you persist in hounding us? How did you know where we were?"

The man answered the last question first. "When I came to, I asked around. Someone had seen you come in here. So I fetched a couple of my pards and came back to take up where I left off."

"Can't you let us be?" Delicia said testily. "You're the one who started it, after all."

"No, this tub of lard did," the man replied, jabbing a thumb at Rupert. Then he gingerly touched his temple. "Thanks to your pa, my head is pounding something fierce."

"Thanks to me," Fargo corrected him, swiveling so he faced all three. None of them appeared to have noticed that his right hand remained under the table. "And I can do it again if you want."

"I'd like to see you try!" the ruffian blustered. "No one gets the better of Ike Talbot twice." Talbot's hand drifted toward the butt of his Remington but he froze when he heard a distinct metallic click. Glancing down, he swallowed hard, his Adam's apple bobbing. "Is that what I think it is?"

"Try to unlimber your hardware and you'll find out," Fargo said. "I want all three of you to unbuckle your gunbelts and let them drop. Then light a shuck or I'll put windows in your skulls."

Delicia rose, saying, "Maybe it would be better if we were the ones who left. We're done eating anyway. And I'd rather avoid trouble if at all possible." Gripping her father's sleeve, she headed for the entrance.

Fargo would rather it was the other way around, but he did as she requested, covering the three cutthroats with his Colt as he backed toward the door. Delicia paid the waitress, and within moments they were squinting in the bright glare of the mid-morning sun. Fargo holstered his Colt but kept one eye on the restaurant as they bore to the left and blended in among scores of bustling pedestrians.

"Why is that dreadful man so determined to do me harm?" Rupert said. "All I did was bump into him."

"Didn't you smell his breath?" Fargo rejoined. "He's half drunk, and snake-mean.

He likes to cause trouble and you've given him an excuse."

"But I apologized."

"That doesn't matter." Fargo figured the professor would never fully understand. East of the Mississippi violence was the exception, not the rule. But on the frontier, violence was woven into the fabric of everyday life. Violent men were everywhere, spawned in part by the savage wilderness they called home and in part by the savagery lurking in the depths of their own dark souls. Most easterners found it difficult to believe that there were people who *liked* to hurt others, people who could kill another human being as casually as they swatted a fly.

"I apologized," Rupert said again, more to himself than to either of them.

"You could say you're sorry from now until doomsday and it wouldn't change a thing," Fargo said. "Talbot is out for blood. Yours."

"He's a filthy beast," Delicia said in disgust.

"A rabid wolf is more like it." Fargo still watched the restaurant. "And there are a lot more in Denver just like him."

Rupert gazed up and down the street. "Where's a constable when we need one? In Atlanta there's one every few blocks."

The professor continued to judge the frontier by civilized standards, Fargo mused. There was just one overworked marshal in Denver, but he couldn't be everywhere at once. Rumor had it there was a move afoot to have half a dozen deputies appointed but so far nothing had come of the idea, thanks to certain vested criminal interests determined to keep it from happening.

As they rounded a corner, heading in the general direction of the Grand Hotel, Fargo allowed himself to relax. Talbot and company weren't following. Still, to be on the safe side, he offered, "I'll see you all the way to your hotel."

"Why, how gallant of you." Delicia, displaying those pearly teeth of hers, hooked a slender arm in his. "You're a perfect gentleman."

"Only in public," Fargo said to test her reaction, and was pleased when she laughed lustily instead of being offended.

Leaning toward him, her breast brushing against his elbow, Delicia impishly whispered in his ear, "And how, pray tell, do you act in private?"

Professor Cadwell clucked like an irate hen. "Behave yourself, daughter." To Fargo, he said, "You must forgive her. Their mother died when my darling daughters were quite young, and I'm afraid I've been remiss in instilling moral virtue."

"In other words," Delicia teased, "my own father thinks I'm a shameless hussy."

"Not shameless, no," Rupert said.

Ahead was an alley. Fargo was so intent on the vision of loveliness at his side that he neglected to give it the attention it deserved. It was an oversight he regretted when they started to walk past it and the barrel of a revolver was roughly jammed into the base of his spine.

"Not a peep out of any of you," Ike Talbot warned.

One of Talbot's friends seized Rupert, the other grabbed Delicia. Fingers grasped the collar of Fargo's buckskin shirt and he was pulled into the alleyway after them. If any of the passersby observed what was happening, none voiced an objection.

Empty crates, refuse, and a broken wagon wheel littered the alley. Fargo was shoved against a wall, jarring his chest and chin and nearly losing his hat. Talbot relieved him of the Colt, then stepped back.

"You can turn around now, mister, and get your due."

Rupert and Delicia were next to a crate, the father's arm protectively draped over his daughter's shoulder. In front of them, fists clenched, were Talbot's partners, poised like grizzlies eager to rip and rend.

"You really didn't think I'd let you get the drop on me and not do anything about it, did you, mister?" Talbot addressed Fargo. "Once word got around, I'd never be able to show my face in Denver again."

Rupert had more grit than most would in his situation. "Your juvenile posturing is grating on my nerves, sir! Were I ten years younger, I'd thrash you within an inch of your life."

Talbot nodded at the tallest of his friends, who immediately buried a fist in the professor's stomach. Rupert doubled over, wheezing and sputtering, his eyes filling with tears and spittle dribbling over his lower lip.

"You bastards!" Delicia screeched, throwing herself at her father's attacker, her fingernails hooked to rake his face. But the man back-handed her across the cheek, slamming her into the crate.

Rage gushed through Fargo and he started to take a step, stopping when Talbot cocked the Remington. It took all of Fargo's self-control not to throw caution to the breeze and tear into him.

"I wouldn't if'n I were you. There are three of us, remember?"

Fargo had to lure the three men closer. Sneering, he said, "Three cowards who hit women and beat older men. What else do you do to prove how tough you are? Kick puppies and spit on babies?"

Talbot's features twisted in spite. "Another word out of you and you'll be laid up for a month of Sundays."

"Big talk for someone with a yellow streak down his back." Fargo's plan to provoke them into coming closer worked better than he had counted on. For in the very next moment, Talbot hissed like a rattler, gestured at his companions, and all three rushed him.

2

Skye Fargo dropped into a crouch and raised his left arm over his head as if to protect himself from the combined assault of the three men. He wanted to give the impression he was cowering in fear, to make them think he wouldn't fight back. But nothing could be further from the truth.

Tensing both legs, Fargo dipped his right hand into his boot and palmed the Arkansas toothpick nestled snug in its ankle sheath. A quick tug, and the slim knife was free. Fargo waited until the last split second, when the trio were right on top of him and about to pummel him into submission. Then he surged upward, lashing out, his boot catching one of the roughnecks in the groin, his left fist clipping another on the jaw. In almost the same instant Fargo swept his knife in a tight arc, the steel shearing into Ike Talbot's wrist.

Ike howled and backpedaled, dropping both pistols to grasp at his arm, his fingers splayed over the spurting wound.

The other two men glanced at Talbot. Their moment of distraction enabled Fargo to take a step and punch one full in the mouth. As the last hardcase pivoted toward him, Fargo smashed the toothpick's hilt against his ear. Both men folded, one with pulped lips and broken teeth, the other writhing in agony.

But Talbot still had fight left in him. Snarling like an enraged beast, he lunged at his own

Remington lying in the dirt. His outstretched fingers were inches from it when Fargo sliced him across the back of the hand. More blood spurted. Retreating against the other wall, Talbot pressed his arm against his side and grimaced. "Damn your hide! I'll bleed to death!"

Fargo's own blood was boiling. The only thing that kept him from burying the toothpick in Talbot's chest right then and there was the fact that the trio had only intended to beat him into the ground, not kill him. "There's a sawbones two blocks west of here. Get there fast enough and he'll sew you back up."

"You haven't heard the last of me," Talbot declared.

Taking a swift bound, Fargo pressed the bloody blade against Talbot's throat. "If you try anything like this again, I won't hold back. The next time they'll plant you on boot hill. Savvy?"

Talbot, glowering, nodded curtly. "I savvy, sure enough, you son of a bitch."

Fargo shoved him toward the alley's mouth, then did likewise with Talbot's two friends. Several pedestrians had stopped to watch, among them a dapper man in an expensive suit and high hat. He first stared at the scarlet staining Talbot's arm, then at the blood oozing over the chin of the man Fargo had punched, then at Fargo. "Stranger, you're made a grievous mistake. Perhaps you haven't heard. We don't tolerate this sort of rowdy behavior in Denver."

"They started it," Fargo said, then he angrily motioned. "Get the hell out of here, all of you. This doesn't concern you."

"That's where you're wrong," the dandy declared. "Mark my words. Certain steps will be taken." With that puzzling comment, he left, along with everyone else.

Talbot and his cronies also shuffled off, Talbot throwing a last sneering glance at them that hinted more trouble was to come. Some men, and Talbot apparently was one of them, were too hardheaded for their own good. Fargo hoped he was wrong, though, and that Talbot would just let it drop.

A groan brought Fargo's attention over to Rupert, who was still bent over and gasping like a fish out of water. "Do you need a doctor too?"

"No." The professor huffed. "Give me a minute to compose myself. He hit me right in the stomach. And after that pie I ate—" Rupert closed his eyes and sagged against the wall. "I must say, this city is beginning to lose some of its appeal. Why do they allow thugs like that to roam at large?"

Fargo didn't answer. But the professor didn't know the half of it. Denver was a hotbed of violence, crawling with every vice known to man—and then some. The city fathers tried to confine the worst of the law-lessness to a bawdy district bordered by Holiday, Blake, and Larimer streets. The former, in particular, was a den of footpads, swindlers, owlhoots, and fallen doves. It was nicknamed "the street of a thousand sinners," and the crusading publisher of the *Rocky Mountain News* had once written that the four-block area "held more prostitute flesh, saw more wickedness, and more sin than any four other blocks" in the entire West.

Not that Fargo minded a little wildness. He liked to drink. He liked to gamble. And as for fallen doves, he was on a first-name basis with more than he cared to count. What some church-goers branded as sinning, he called living. But he could do without the cheats and cardsharps, the thieves and cutthroats, and the cold-blooded killers who prowled the bawdy district in search of prey.

Delicia looped an arm around her father's waist. "Are you sure we shouldn't get you to a doctor? You might be bleeding inside."

"I'll be fine in a minute or two," Rupert said, patting her hand. He looked at Fargo. "Again we are in your debt. If not for you, who knows what those vermin would have done to us. How can we ever repay you?"

"There's no need," Fargo said. Since nothing else was handy, he untied his bandanna and used it to wipe the blood from the Arkansas toothpick. Replacing the knife in its sheath, he reclaimed his Colt. Then he picked up Talbot's Remington and held it out to the professor. "Maybe you should hold on to this. Just in case."

Rupert shook his head. "I've never shot a gun in my life. I'm afraid I'd be more likely to blow my own foot off than hit someone else."

"I'll take it," Delicia surprised them both by saying, and snatched the heavy pistol.

21

Grasping it in both hands, she sighted down the barrel. "All I need to do is pull the trigger, right?"

"No, it's a single-action revolver," Fargo said. "You have to pull back the hammer first, then squeeze off a shot." He paused. "You've never fired a gun before, either, I take it?"

"Of course not. The only vermin I had to fend off in Atlanta were lechers, and usually a slap or two was all it took." Delicia's rosy lips quirked upward. "If that didn't do the trick, a knee to their manhood invariably did."

"Only use the pistol if you have no other choice, then," Fargo suggested. "Aim at their chest, not at their arms or legs or head. You're less likely to miss. Stroke the trigger when you fire, don't jerk it. And remember, the gun will kick some."

Rupert straightened. "I really wish you would give it back to Mr. Fargo, my dear. I'm uncomfortable around firearms."

"What if Talbot pays us another visit?" Delicia argued. "And what if Skye isn't around to protect us?" She wagged the Remington. "This will discourage him." Opening her traveling bag, she shoved the pistol in.

Fargo escorted them as far as the lobby of the Grand Hotel. Rupert said he was in dire need of a nap and headed up the carpeted stairs. Delicia lingered a moment, offering her hand in parting.

"I do so hope we meet again. I've enjoyed your company immensely, and I'd like to get to know you a lot better."

The feeling was mutual. Fargo watched

her sashay off, the enticing sway of her hips and the outline of her long legs against her dress enough to make his mouth go dry with anticipation. Sighing wistfully, he left and threaded through the streets to his favorite haunt, the Palace Saloon. Its name was glitzier than its trappings. Ordering a glass of whiskey, Fargo strolled to the gaming tables and sat in on a game of five-card stud. He had about twelve dollars to his name and he hoped to double it. Lady Luck, however, had deserted him; an hour after sunset he was down to only two, which would barely cover the stable fee he had to pay. And there was still his hotel bill.

Mulling over what to do, Fargo ambled to his own hotel, Long's Peak. It was in a seamier district, a part of town decent folks generally avoided after dark. But the bedding was clean and a fresh basin of water was provided daily. Fargo nodded at the desk clerk then trudged up to his second-floor room. Although it was early yet, he decided to turn in. In the morning he would wrestle with the problem of his finances, such as they were.

Fargo turned the key and was opening the door when a faint scrape from within brought him up short. Someone was inside! Suddenly he thought of the rather furtive glance the clerk had given him. He started to back down the hall but halted on hearing the tramp of boots on the stairs.

"Shouldn't we wait for the signal?" a muffled voice asked.

"No, they're bound to have him by now."

Fargo was stunned to see four men in black

hoods appear on the landing. At the sight of him, they stopped. Then one lifted a shotgun and shouted.

"B.B! He's out here! He's spotted us!"

Whirling, Fargo raced down the corridor. As he flew past his room, the door was flung open and another hooded figure materialized, holding a cane. He thrust it at Fargo's legs in an effect to trip him but Fargo was too quick. Leaping over the outstretched cane, he sped to the window at the far end. Thankfully, it wasn't latched. Throwing it open, Fargo leaned out. Below was a dark side street.

Fargo glanced back, seeing nine or ten hooded men bearing down on him. Sliding a leg over the sill, he slid out, gripping the sill with both hands, dangled a moment, then dropped—just as rough hands sought to ensnare his wrists.

"Damn!" someone thundered. "After him! We can't let him get away!"

Fargo landed hard. Rocked on his heels, he tottered several feet before he regained his balance. A hooded head had poked out the window. Spinning, Fargo ran. He didn't know who they were or why they were after him, and he wasn't sticking around to find out. They struck him as the kind who would shoot first and explain later.

"He's heading south!" the man at the window screeched. "Travis, you and your men cut him off!"

Fargo had only gone about fifteen feet when more hooded apparitions appeared up ahead, all armed with rifles or shotguns.

Stopping, Fargo turned to retrace his steps. A tremendous din in the hotel confirmed the others were barreling after him. People were yelling out of their rooms, demanding to know what all the ruckus was about. The next second the rear door to the hotel opened, disgorging more shadowy shapes in black hoods.

Fargo was trapped! Or was he? To his right was a high fence, to his left an empty yard choked by weeds. He raced across it, then around a frame house, ending up on a wider street. Somewhere a dog commenced barking, which set others to doing the same. Fargo ran to the west, seeking to outdistance his pursuers.

Heartbeats later, hooded men spilled around both sides of the frame house. "There he is!" one shouted, and the rest gave immediate chase.

His legs pumping, Fargo held to a steady sprint for several blocks. The farther he traveled, the fewer lights and pedestrians he encountered. He gained ground on the masked mob, but not by much, certainly not enough to insure his escape. At the next intersection he jogged northward.

Two blocks off, a small carriage was clattering toward him. Fargo came to a halt in the inky gloom, next to a waist-high picket fence. On impulse, he vaulted over it and flattened in the shrubbery beyond.

Just as he did, the pack poured around the corner. There were fifteen or more, all told, and in their vanguard was the man with the mahogany cane. They looked every which way. As they came abreast of the picket fence, they slowed, then stopped, many puffing as if they had run ten miles.

"Where did he get to?"

"He came this way. We all saw him."

The man at the forefront held his cane aloft. "Quiet! We'll find out in a second."

A block off, the driver had brought the carriage to a halt and was sitting there, staring in bewilderment.

"Did you see a big fellow in buckskins run by?" the man with the cane called out.

"No, sir. I sure didn't." The driver sounded scared. "You're those vigilantes, aren't you? The ones I've been reading about in the newspaper?"

"That we are, my good man," the cane wielder replied. "But you need not fear on our account. We're the scourge of the criminal element, the riffraff and the bummers. Not decent fellows like yourself."

Fargo was trying to make sense of what he'd just heard. Vigilantes? In Denver? And they were after *him*? What in the world for? He hadn't committed any crimes. He reasoned there must be a mistake, but he wasn't about to stand up and say so. Not with all those nervous fingers on the triggers of all those shotguns and rifles. They would blow him apart if he so much as let out a peep.

"You can be on your way," the man holding the cane directed the driver. "We won't detain you."

With a light flick of the driver's whip, the

horse moved forward. The bay came on slowly, the skittish driver looking as if he would rather be anywhere than where he was. "I don't want no trouble," he said to the gathered men. The carriage was actually a coupe, a shorter, cut-off version more commonly found in places like New Orleans and San Francisco. It sported a curved front glass, glass side windows, and a single wide seat for up to three occupants.

The vigilante with the cane faced his followers. "Let it go by, boys. Then we'll search every square foot of this block. If our quarry resists, shoot him dead."

Fargo had to get out of there. But he didn't dare show himself. He debated whether to try and crawl off. Then the advancing coupe gave him an idea. The vigilantes were moving to the other side of the street to permit it to pass. Soon it would be between them and the picket fence. With every nerve tingling, Fargo eased up into a crouch.

The driver couldn't take his eyes off the hooded avengers. A sickly smile creasing his craggy face, he kept saying to the bay, "Nice and slow. Nice and slow."

Fargo focused on the near door. The moment the horse screened him from the view of his pursuers, he leaped the fence, bent low, and darted to the coupe. A twist of the latch and he had the door open. Placing both hands on the floor, he levered himself inside. In the murk he didn't see the carriage's occupant until he bumped against a soft, yielding body. There was a low gasp of shock and the rustle of a dress.

"Don't make a sound!" Fargo warned, clamping a hand over a pair of full lips. Peering out, he saw the vigilantes impatiently waiting for the coupe to go by. He was glad they didn't have torches or lanterns, or they would spot him right away.

The driver cracked his whip again and the coupe picked up speed. Fargo pulled the door quietly shut and sat back, sliding his hand off the passenger's mouth. "I'm sorry," he said. "But I couldn't let you give me away."

A throaty chuckle was her reaction. "I'll say this for you, friend. You sure know how to get a girl's blood flowing." She leaned toward him, betraying no fear. "What was that all about, anyhow?"

Fargo inhaled the scent of flowery perfume. She was a brunette in her early thirties, if he was any judge, and quite attractive. An oval face distinguished by a pert, upturned nose and exquisite lips added to her appeal. "I wish I knew," he answered. "They were waiting for me in my hotel room."

"The Committee," the woman said with a tinge of contempt.

"Who?"

"You must be new in town," she said. "They call themselves the Committee of Safety. One hundred of the most upstanding, prominent citizens in all of Denver. About a month ago they took to hanging and shooting murderers and thieves. Others they've driven out with a warning."

"You don't sound very fond of them."

"I'm not." The woman sat back, at ease

now that she knew Fargo wouldn't harm her. "I'm Rosie O'Grady, by the way. I work at Jennie Roger's House of Mirrors. Maybe you've heard of it?"

Most men had. The House of Mirrors had a justly earned reputation for being heaven on earth. As plush as a sultan's palace, it ranked with Paradise Alley, Club Annex, The Fashion, and Mattie Silk's as one of the top bawdy houses in the city. "That I have," Fargo acknowledged, regarding her in a whole new light. Rosie's dress had been tailored to accent her many feminine charms, from the sensational sweep of her full breasts to the sultry enchantment of her crossed thighs.

"The Committee must be after you for a reason, handsome," she commented. "Have you killed anyone recently? Or maybe robbed somebody?"

"I'm no footpad," Fargo said, a trifle indignantly. "And no, I haven't killed anyone in two or three weeks."

"That long, huh?" Rosie chuckled. "Well, if you want my advice, you'll sneak out of town tomorrow and head for parts unknown. The Committee has a long reach. And if they mean to bury you, they won't rest until they do."

Now there was comforting news, Fargo reflected. "I don't know what I'll do," he absently responded.

"Do you have anywhere safe to spend the night? If not, you're welcome to sleep at my place."

Fargo glanced at her. In the shadowed

confines of the coupe it was difficult to read her expression. "You'd do that for someone you've just met? A total stranger?"

"Anyone the Committee is after automatically earns my sympathy," Rosie said. "A couple of weeks ago they dragged a good friend of mine from his bed in the middle of the night. His name was Halloran, and he was a gambler. Not the most honest of gamblers, mind you, but he never hurt anyone, never swindled helpless spinsters out of their life savings or anything like that."

"What did the vigilantes do to him?"

"They hung him from a tree along Cherry Creek. Right where the main road enters Denver so everyone who went by could see him hanging there with a board around his neck. 'Death to all bummers,' they wrote on it."

"Bummers?"

"That's their name for those they consider common riffraff. Bummers, or bums, the Committee calls them." Rosie uttered a soft string of swear words. "They're all a bunch of hypocrites, if you ask me. And I ought to know. I've bedded some of them. Afterward they slink on back to their wives and strut around pretending they're decent, upstanding paragons of virtue. But I know better."

"Your name isn't on their list?" Fargo said, jesting, but she took him seriously.

"Not that I know of. They haven't strung up any women yet. But give them time. As I said, they've only been in business about a month. Each week they get bolder. Before long

30

they'll probably be parading through the streets in broad daylight, shooting anyone who looks at them crosswise."

From where Fargo sat, he could see the back of the driver. When the man shifted and bent down, Fargo promptly ducked as low as he could, pressing against Rosie's legs.

"Who are you jabbering to down there, lady?"

"No one, you yack," Rosie answered. "Who would I be talking to? I'm the only one in here. Or have you forgotten?"

"I'd swear I heard voices."

"It's that flask you keep sipping out of," Rosie said. "I'd be hearing voices too if I was half soused."

"I am not!" the driver declared. "Being pickled on the job is grounds for being fired. Sure, I take a nip against the chill now and then. But I can drive as straight and true as you or anyone else."

"Then prove it. Get me to my house in one piece and maybe I won't file a complaint with the company you work for."

The driver straightened, and Rosie giggled girlishly. "I guess I told him. You can sit up now, handsome," she whispered.

Fargo did, but as he rose the coupe took a sharp turn, pitching him against her. They were nose to nose, virtually mouth to mouth, Rosie's breath warm on his face, her eyes twinkling pinpoints of amusement.

"Well, you work fast, don't you?"

"It was an accident."

"Really? More's the pity." Grinning, Rosie

kissed him full on the mouth, the tip of her tongue rimming his lips in a delicious tease.

Fargo slid onto the seat, close beside her, but not close enough because she wriggled her bottom sideways until her thigh brushed his. "Not the shy type, are you?"

"In my line of work?" Rosie started to laugh, then stifled herself with a palm. Regaining her composure, she whispered, "No, I'm not. And if I don't mind, why should you? All my life people have criticized me for being too forward. My mother, my grandmother, my sisters, my cousins. If I had a dollar for every time they accused me of being too friendly with the opposite sex, I'd have more money than John Jacob Astor."

Astor, who made a fortune in the fur trade, was at one time the richest man in America. "Don't get me wrong," Fargo said softly. "I don't hold it against you."

"You don't, but those vigilantes would. It's not fair, I tell you."

"How so?"

"People like that have the same urges we do, the same needs. They like to enjoy themselves as much as the rest of us. Yet they look down their noses at people like you and me because we don't live up to the standards they've set, standards even they can't live up to. It makes no sense to me." Rosie took a deep breath. "Sorry to climb on my pulpit. But where the Committee of Safety is concerned, it doesn't take much to get my dander up. Now, how about my invitation?"

"What happens to you if they catch us together?" This was Fargo's chief worry.

"Who cares? If they try to run me out of Denver, I'll threaten to make a list of all the holier-than-thou citizens who frequent the houses of ill repute and post copies all over the city. That will teach the bastards!"

It could also get her killed, which Fargo mentioned, adding, "If they find us, I'll tell them I forced you to hide me at gunpoint. I don't want you harmed on my account."

Rosie recoiled, as if greatly surprised, then smiled sweetly and traced his jaw with a fingertip. "That's about the nicest thing anyone ever said to me." She pecked him on the chin. "I'm beginning to think I'm dreaming this whole thing, or you're a figment of my imagination. You're about everything a gal could wish for in a man."

"You've only known me five minutes," Fargo noted.

The coupe began to slow and Rosie glanced out the window. "Oh, my. We're almost there. The driver is bound to see you unless I can keep his attention on me." She fiddled with her hat. "Wait until it's safe. Then come on around to the back of my house. I'll be waiting."

"Whoa, there, Molly!" they heard the driver say.

Fargo hunched close to the floor, his hand on the Colt.

Rosie stood even before the man yanked open the door. "Help a lady down, why don't you?" she requested.

The driver complied, closing the door again without looking in.

"Would you mind walking me to my porch? I hate to be a burden, but just last week a woman down the street was molested."

"If you asked real nice-like, I'd walk you clear to your bedroom," the driver said.

"Now, now. Behave or I'll strangle you with your own pecker."

Fargo rose up high enough to watch them move toward a modest house set well back from the street. Slipping out, he crept around to the rear of the coupe and hunkered down.

Rosie paid the driver and went in. The man dallied, hoping, no doubt, she would take him up on his suggestion, but when a minute went by and she didn't return, he frowned and stomped up into the carriage. "Women!" he muttered, snaking his whip at the tired bay.

Fargo stayed where he was until the night swallowed him. Heeding Rosie's instructions, he hurried to the back door and rapped lightly, twice. When it opened, he gazed in amazement. Somehow, in that short amount of time, she had changed from her dress into a lacy gown.

"See anything you like, big man?"

3

"Come in," Rosie O'Grady bid Skye Fargo. "I bet you can use a drink."

Fargo's mouth had gone dry, although not from thirst. He followed her into a small but comfortable parlor, feasting on the enticing contours of her lush body. She was shorter than he by a good foot and a half, every part superbly proportioned. Her legs and her buttocks were marble smooth and firm, her breasts twin peaks waiting to be scaled. He saw that her nipples were set higher than most and pointed almost straight up in tempting invitation.

Rosie took a decanter from a cabinet and filled a glass. "Scotch," she said. "It's all I have on hand at the moment. I hope it will do."

"It will," Fargo said, downing it in two gulps. The liquor scorched a path to the pit of his stomach, warming his insides. Removing his hat and gunbelt, he placed them on an oak table. "I want to thank you for helping me."

"To be honest, I might not have if you weren't such a good-looking devil. I took a shine to you right away." Moving nearer, Rosie placed her hands on his broad shoulders. "And I hope the feeling is mutual."

Fargo let his actions answer her. Sliding an arm around her waist, he molded her to his body, his mouth descending to cover hers. Their tongues entwined in an erotic caress, causing her breath to flutter in her throat. She squirmed when he covered a breast with his other hand and gently kneaded it, her nipple hardening against his palm.

"Oh, my," Rosie husked when they broke for air. "I knew you'd be special, but I had no idea how special." She kissed his neck, his chin, her hands exploring his arms and torso. "My goodness, you have a lot of muscles. You must do a lot of outdoor work."

Fargo fused his mouth to hers again. Their lips were molten fire. She panted through her nose, her legs wriggling against his as he roved his hand down her back, over the lacy gown, and cupped her bottom. She was hot down there, as well.

"Ohhh," Rosie moaned when they parted. "Come with me." Clasping his hand, she led him down a short hall to a tastefully decorated bedroom. Like the rest of the house, it was small, and there was barely room for the double-sized bed. A mauve quilt complemented the purple drapes covering the window. Rosie's discarded dress and hat lay on the floor at the foot of the bed, and she now added her lacy nightgown to the pile.

"This place isn't much, I know," Rosie said, "but it's all mine. I scrimped and saved for ages to come up with the down payment. Another five years and I'll have it all paid off."

"Rosie, I should tell you," Fargo said. "I don't have much—" She didn't let him finish.

Pressing a finger over his mouth, Rosie wagged a finger. "Did I ask for any? Don't insult me. This isn't for money. This is for me."

Rosie climbed onto the bed and pulled him on beside her. "What do you think? It's the softest one I could find."

Fargo's knees sank inches into the mattress. He stretched out beside her and kissed her throat and her ear while her fingers pried at his belt buckle, loosening it. When his buckskin pants parted, she brazenly slid a hand into them.

At the first electric contact, Fargo stiffened. In more ways than one. His pole surged and swelled, becoming iron as she rubbed him from top to bottom. She knew just how to do it, just where to touch, to pleasure a man most. She wasn't too rough, as some women would be. An involuntary moan escaped him.

"Like that, do you?" Rosie teased. "Most men do. But you haven't seen anything yet. The best is yet to come." Bending, she lowered her head.

Fargo closed his eyes, savoring the sensations her molten lips and gliding tongue provoked. Her experience showed in her deft manipulation of his organ, in her ability to arouse him to new heights.

Women like Rosie were all too rare. Women who enjoyed sharing their bodies without reservation or embarrassment. The sad truth was that too many were too prudish to fully enjoy themselves when they made love. From childhood they were raised to believe that touching a man was sinful, that allowing a man to touch them was even worse. It affected their entire lives. When they made love, they did so timidly, with fear gnawing at their hearts, afraid to fully enjoy themselves, afraid to let themselves do all the things they secretly longed to do for fear of overstepping the bounds imposed by their upbringing. Some women wouldn't think of touching a man below his belt, let alone kissing him there.

So for the longest while Fargo lay on his back relishing Rosie's manipulation. Tension drained from him like water from a sieve. Stirring, he tugged her arms to get her attention, then motioned for her to swing her body around, which she eagerly did. Her thighs were now on either side of his head, her womanhood inches away. He inhaled the dank scent of her core, then applied his mouth to her slit. She was wet, dripping wet, and at the first flick of his tongue on her swollen knob she arched her back and uttered a low cry.

Fargo licked her moist edges and tasted her salty essence. Rosie's legs enfolded his head and she ground her bottom into him to heighten her excitement. She cried out once more when he delved his tongue deeper.

"Oh! Oh! Yes, Skye! Yes!"

For minutes on end Fargo did to her as she had done to him. Her inner walls rippled and contracted as he licked and sucked and lathered her core. Suddenly she exploded, her whole body quaking and shaking as she clung to him in a delirium of ecstasy.

Eventually Rosie coasted to a stop and lay mewing like a kitten. Fargo rolled her onto her back and rotated so he was between her knees. His engorged, bulging manhood was purple with lust, anxious to taste the same treats his mouth had. Gripping it, he rubbed himself along her opening, eliciting a drawn-out groan. Then, ever so slowly, inch by gradual inch, he inserted himself to the hilt.

"Ahhh! So nice! So big!"

Rosie's nails bit into his back as she planted kisses on his chest, his shoulders, his neck. At his initial thrust she flung her head back, her mouth wide, her eyes wider.

"Yesssssssss! Take me Skye! Please, take me!"

Fargo wasn't about to rush. He settled into a steady but slow rhythm, his hips bucking up and in, up and in. For her part, Rosie matched him, driving her hips against his at the same tempo. Fargo tweaked her nipples, pulling on them to arouse her further. Her gasps and coos were constant. Her legs wrapped around his waist for added leverage, and she gripped his biceps with both hands.

"You're the best," Rosie breathed. "The best ever."

Fargo doubted it, but he was flattered nonetheless and determined to take her over the brink. His thrusts grew in force and urgency. Underneath them the bed bounced and creaked, the racket growing louder as the speed of their coupling increased. Fargo sucked on her tongue, on her nipples. She ran her hands through his hair, across his chest, down around to his lower back.

"Almost there! Almost!"

So was Fargo. He held off as long as he could, the creaking and rattling of the bed reaching a crescendo. It was a wonder it didn't fall apart altogether. Fargo pressed down on her shoulders and rammed himself upward.

"Now!" Rosie screamed. "Now! Now! Now!"

Fargo felt her release, and her orgasm spurred his own release. Another couple of strokes and he erupted like a volcano, spewing endlessly, it seemed, his vision blurring as the bedroom spun. His heart hammered. His temples pounded. Pure bliss overcame him, bliss so potent he lost all track of time, all sense of place and being. He was adrift in a sea of undiluted rapture.

Moments like these were what Fargo lived for. Moments when all was right with the world, when he was transported beyond himself. But, like all such moments, it came to an end. In due course Fargo floated down to earth and became aware of the bed, of the rumpled quilt, and of Rosie's perspiring body under his own, of her heavy breathing. He rolled onto his back.

"Lordy! If more men made love like you do, there wouldn't be any spinsters."

Chuckling, Fargo placed a hand on her stomach, which fluttered at his touch. "It's my way of thanking you," he joked.

"Is that so? Then I'll wake you in the morning so you can thank me again. And again. And again."

They laughed and embraced. Fargo was lowering his mouth to hers when a soft thump sounded from the front of the house.

Rosie tensed. "Did you hear that?"

Nodding, Fargo rolled off the bed. He buckled

his pants, then moved to the doorway. The house was quiet but he had an uneasy feeling. He wished he hadn't left his gunbelt out in the parlor. "Do you have a gun in here?"

"No. I never have one around. Some of my men friends drink a little too much and might be tempted to shoot up the place." Rosie sat up and pulled the quilt up around her shoulders.

"Stay here," Fargo cautioned. Gliding down the hall, he told himself that there must be a perfectly logical explanation for the noise, that maybe a knickknack had fallen off a shelf or the wind had blown a tree limb against the house. But deep down he knew he was deceiving himself. He already knew what he would find when he reached the parlor.

Six hooded figures were waiting for him, three armed with leveled shotguns, the rest holding rifles. A seventh, the man with the cane, sat in a chair by the table. Tapping Fargo's gunbelt with it, he said, "Extremely careless of you, wouldn't you agree?"

It would do no good for Fargo to try and escape. He couldn't dodge buckshot. And the only place to retreat to was back to the bedroom, which would endanger Rosie. Holding his arms out from his sides, he moved to the table.

"Wise decision," the vigilantes' leader remarked. "Running would only get you killed that much sooner. Our men have the house surrounded. There's one or two at each window and both doors, just waiting for you to show your face."

"What the hell do you want?" Fargo demanded. He was tired of being chased, of being treated like a common thug.

"We want you," the leader said. "I suppose you know who we are?"

"You're vigilantes. You're cowards who hide behind masks so you can't be brought to justice yourselves." Fargo didn't hide his scorn.

One of the others cursed and hiked his shotgun as if to bash the stock against Fargo's temple, but the leader waved his cane.

"No, Joseph. We're not barbarians, despite what this man seems to think." He paused. "I can see an explanation is in order. But first, Joseph, go tell Miss O'Grady she has twenty-four hours to leave the city or she will find herself behind bars."

"No," Fargo said, barring Joseph's way.

"No?" the leader repeated. "You must be under the impression that you have a say in these matters. You don't."

"Why punish her?" Fargo responded. "She hasn't done anything. I made her bring me here."

"And you also made her make love to you?" The leader snickered. "Based on what we heard, I'd say she was a willing participant." Some of the vigilantes thought the comment was hilarious.

"So what if she was?" Fargo countered. "If you run her out of Denver, you might as well run out every fallen dove. Singling her out wouldn't be right. She likes it here. She even bought this house with her own money."

"Do tell?" The leader leaned on his cane.

"Very well. Joseph, instruct Miss O'Grady to stay in her room until we're gone. And to keep her mouth shut afterward." As the one called Joseph passed Fargo, their leader gestured at the sofa. "Please. Have a seat. We need to talk."

Fargo obliged, acutely conscious of the shotguns fixed on his midsection. "For a vigilante, you sure are polite."

"We're not the monsters some portray us as. I'll prove it to you." The leader set his cane across his lap and removed his hood, revealing a lantern-jawed face marked by a stern mouth and high forehead. "Now do you know who I am?"

Fargo did indeed. William Newton Byers. Byers was the owner and editor of the *Rocky Mountain News,* and one of Denver's most distinguished citizens. Fargo had seen Byers a few times, but had never met him personally. "You've gone from writing the news to making it, is that the general idea?"

"Not hardly." Byers ran a hand through his shock of dark hair, then scratched his neck. "These damnable hoods itch something awful. But it is essential we keep our identities secret. Our enemies will stop at nothing to bury us, including shooting or knifing us in the back if they knew who we were."

"Who are these enemies you keep mentioning?"

Byers scowled. "Surely you've heard about the bummers? The no-good hellions who have terrorized this city since its inception? Their leader is Charley Harrison. Are you familiar with the scoundrel?"

"I've heard of him," Fargo admitted. As had anyone who stayed in Denver any length of time. Harrison was a gambler by trade. He owned the roughest saloon in the city, and had a reputation for being extremely deadly with a gun or knife.

"Harrison is the Devil Incarnate. Did you know that he had boasted he wants to kill at least twelve white men before he dies so he'll have a jury of his peers in hell?"

"Some men like to talk big," Fargo said.

"Charley Harrison does more than talk. He's appointed himself the crime boss of the city. He controls most of the brothels and many of the saloons. All he has to do is snap his fingers and his men will dispose of anyone he wishes. Why, just one month ago Harrison coldly murdered a man who wanted to sit in on a poker game he was involved in for no other reason than the man was a good poker player and Harrison didn't feel like losing."

"Why didn't the marshal arrest him?"

"Because half a dozen of Harrison's despicable underlings were willing to testify the other man was to blame. Willing to lie under oath that Harrison shot him in self-defense. There was nothing the marshal could do." Byers paused. "It was the straw that broke the camel's back. Harrison and his cutthroats pose a grave threat to the future prosperity of our fair city, and I, for one, won't stand idly by while they tear down everything we've worked so hard to build up."

Fargo glanced at the other vigilantes. "So you've taken the law into your own hands."

44

"What else were we to do? Permit Harrison and his ilk to ride roughshod over the entire populace? We are family men, Mr. Fargo. We have a responsibility to our loved ones to defend them and our investments to the best of our ability. Since the law is powerless, we're dealing with the problem in our own fashion."

"By hanging and shooting men without giving them a chance to defend themselves? Without giving them a fair trial?"

"Oh, they have fair hearings, I can promise you that. We conduct private courts, complete with witnesses and testimony. We've never hung anyone on hearsay or circumstantial evidence. Only the guilty."

"In your eyes."

Byers was annoyed and it showed. "Who are you to judge us? Do you live here? Do you have a wife or children? No, you don't. So you don't need to contend with the countless crimes committed by the bummers on a daily basis." Byers sat up, thunder roiling on his brow. "In the past two years there have been fifteen horrendous murders which we know, beyond a shadow of a doubt, were committed by Harrison's men. Yet we've always lacked the proof necessary to charge them. Should we have let it go on? Where should we draw the line? At twenty murders? At forty? Fifty?"

Fargo made no reply.

"Fault us if you will, but what we have done has been for the betterment of the community and the safety of our families. I don't regret helping to form the Committee of

45

Safety one bit. Rather, I regret not having formed it sooner."

"What do you want with me?" This was the question uppermost on Fargo's mind. "Why were you waiting for me at my hotel?"

"One of the members of our Committee reported that you were involved in a tussle in an alley this morning. Pistols were brandished. A woman was struck—"

Now it was Fargo's turn to show annoyance. "I was protecting her, and her father. If you don't believe me, check with them. Their name is Cadwell. They're staying at the Grand Hotel."

"The Cadwells? An Amity Cadwell visited my office today, inquiring about the latest news from the goldfields."

"She's the older sister of the woman in the alley. It's a good thing she wasn't there, or Ike Talbot and his friends might have assaulted her, too."

One of the vigilantes muttered something inaudible. Another growled like a feral cat. William Byers grasped his cane as if he would like to hit something with it. "So. Mr. Talbot again. He's one of Harrison's henchmen, a lieutenant in Harrison's operation. We suspect him of committing two or three murders."

"Why haven't you strung him up, then?"

"Because he's a wily one. He only roams abroad during the day. At night he holes up with Harrison and a dozen others, all armed to the teeth."

"So where does this leave us?" Fargo wanted to know.

"It leaves me with egg on my face." Grinning, Byers rose and extended his hand. "I trust there will be no hard feelings. I'll spread word among the one hundred, Mr. Fargo, that you are to be left alone." As they shook, Byers's eyes narrowed. "Wait a second. It occurs to me I've heard your name somewhere before." He stiffened. "You're not *the* Skye Fargo?"

"The one and only."

"The famous scout and hunter? The one they call the Trailsman?" Byers slapped himself on the forehead. "Damn me for a simpleton! Why didn't I recognize it sooner? Some of your exploits have appeared in my own newspaper!" He chortled. "Had I realized who you were, none of this would have been necessary. Your reputation, sir, precedes you. They say you're a man of honor and integrity."

Fargo didn't find the misunderstanding anywhere near as humorous. Not when it could have gotten him killed.

"Wait until the rest of the Committee hears this," Byers said. "Why, we might as well have accused Horace Greeley!"

Greeley, the editor of the *New York Tribune,* was widely regarded as one of the most honest, influential journalists in the country. He had visited Denver the year before and had written a glowing testimonial to the growing city.

Fargo, though, never had held a very high opinion of scribblers, as they called themselves. He'd found they tended to exaggerate the facts out of all proportion. Or, as an old stagecoach driver once remarked, "They wouldn't know the truth if it jumped up and bit 'em on the ass."

"Do you mind if I ask what you're doing in our fair city?" Byers asked.

"Trying to stay alive," Fargo rejoined, and rose.

Byers smiled. "I suppose I had that coming. But I would be delighted if you would let me interview you for my paper. Frontiersmen make for good copy, as we say in the trade. Readers love to hear about the adventures of men like Jim Bridger, Kit Carson, and yourself."

"I'll think about it."

"Fair enough. You can reach me at my office." Byers prepared to put his black hood back on.

"One thing, though," Fargo said, as if he'd had an afterthought.

"Yes?"

"About there not being any hard feelings?"

"Yes?"

"You were wrong." Fargo slugged Byers on the jaw. The newspaperman stumbled back against the liquor cabinet and nearly upended it. Two other vigilantes rushed to help him while the others raised their weapons, taking deliberate aim.

"No!" Byers bellowed, rubbing his chin. "I had that coming." He regarded Fargo with icy reserve. "But I won't tolerate a second abuse. Nor will I conduct an interview. Good night, sir." Wheeling, he stalked from the house, the rest of the Committeemen filing out in his wake.

Fargo slammed the door after them and bolted it as Rosie should have done earlier. Strapping on his gunbelt, he verified the Colt was still loaded, then shoved his hat on his head and returned to the bedroom.

Rosie was under the covers, only her fearful face showing. When she saw it was him, she sat up, shamelessly exposing her magnificent breasts. "It's you! I thought you were a goner! How did you talk them out of killing you?"

"I told them they could each have an hour in bed with you," Fargo said, sitting next to her.

Cackling, Rosie hugged him, then lavished his mouth with her velvet tongue. "We're all alone again, handsome, so why don't we take up where we left off?"

"I'd like nothing better," Fargo assured her, "but I have some things to attend to." Such as checking on the Ovaro and insuring the vigilantes hadn't done anything with his personal effects at the hotel.

Rosie was vastly disappointed. "Damn. I like your company, big man. I was hoping we'd see more of each other."

"We will," Fargo promised. "You have my word on that." And he was sincere. He would look her up in a few days and treat her to a night on the town, provided he could get his hands on some money before then.

"I'll be counting the minutes," Rose said lightheartedly, her eyes belying her carefree manner.

Fargo kissed her and left. By his best reckoning it was near on to eleven. The streets in the residential areas were largely deserted, so the odds of finding a carriage for hire were slim. Which was just as well. He didn't have the change to spare for fare anyway.

It took over half an hour for Fargo to reach the stable. The stallion was dozing in its stall. Grains of oats in the feed trough verified it was being fed as he had directed, so Fargo turned around and made for the Long's Peak. The same slight desk clerk who had been on duty when the Committee of Safety paid him a visit was still behind the front desk, reading the *Rocky Mountain News,* of all things.

Fargo had half a mind to drag the man off his stool and give him the same treatment he had given the paper's owner, but he didn't. The clerk couldn't be blamed for being cowed into letting the vigilantes lie in wait.

Taking the stairs two at a time, Fargo warily approached his room. The key was still in the lock, where he'd left it, overlooked by the vigilantes in their haste to catch him. Hand on his Colt, he shoved on the door. Everything was exactly as it should be. His saddlebags, rifles, and bedroll were in the closet, undisturbed.

Shutting the door, Fargo locked it and threw the bolt. Until that moment he hadn't quite realized how tired he was, but now he wanted dearly to stretch out and sleep for hours. Tossing his hat on the dresser, he removed his boots—but not his gunbelt—and plopped onto the bed.

Fargo thought he would drift right off but his mind churned like a windmill in a windstorm. He thought about Delicia. And Rosie. He tried to think of a way to earn some money, fast, and couldn't. Selling the stallion was out of the question. And what use was a horse without a saddle? The only other items of any real value he owned were his pistol and rifle. Of the two, common sense told him it would be better to hold on to the Henry if he planned on venturing back out into the wilderness. But he'd rather not sell either if he could help it. There had to be an alternative.

Weariness finally took its toll. Fargo felt himself drifting off. He was on the verge of falling asleep when a faint sound penetrated his fuzzy consciousness. Listening, he heard it repeated. Something was scratching at his door. Sluggishly, Fargo sat up. He wondered if maybe a cat or dog had wandered into the hotel, and he stood. As he did a new noise sent his blood racing through his veins.

It was the sound of a gun hammer being pulled back.

4

A rush of questions cascaded through Skye Fargo's mind. Had the vigilantes returned? Had striking William Byers turned the fiery crusader against him? Did the Committee of Safety intend to finish what they had started?

Palming the Colt, he eased onto the floor. In his stockinged feet he made no noise as he crept along the wall, avoiding the dresser. Putting an ear to the door, he heard whispers. But he couldn't quite make out what was said.

The knob began to rotate. Someone was testing to see if they could open it. The door creaked as pressure was applied. More whispering ensued. They knew the door was locked and bolted. Their next step would likely be to kick it in and start blasting.

Ever so carefully, Fargo slid the side bolt from the plate. Then he fished in his pocket for the key and inserted it into the lock. He turned the key slowly, waiting for the telltale tiny rasp.

"On the count of three," someone in the corridor said loud enough for Fargo to hear.

Fargo yanked the door open. Poised in the act of lifting a boot was a stocky thug in a flannel shirt. In his right hand he held a Smith & Wesson. Behind him, on either side, were other cutthroats, not one of whom Fargo recognized. For a second the tableau was frozen, the three would-be killers riveted in astonishment. Then they galvanized to life, the man with his foot in the air kicking at Fargo's stomach instead of the door even as he brought the Smith & Wesson to bear.

Fargo fired at near point-blank range, the Colt booming like thunder in the narrow confines. His slug smashed the man backward, into the other two. The man on the right was quickest to recover and leveled a revolver just as Fargo fanned the Colt twice. Hot lead seared the second gunman from sternum to spine and he was flung against the far wall, his back painting a crimson smear as he melted to the floor.

The last killer backpedaled, snapping off two swift shots of his own that bit into the jamb at Fargo's elbow. Fargo responded in kind, a single shot that caught the man high on the left shoulder but didn't drop him.

Firing again, the gunman reached the stairs, turned, and fled.

Fargo gave chase. At the landing he paused, ducking back at the crack of a pistol. The slug smacked into the ceiling. Fargo glimpsed the gunman going around the corner and bounded down to overtake him.

The desk clerk, befuddled by the din, looking as if he had just woke up, jumped to his feet behind the front desk and blurted, "What's this? What's this?"

The last gunman was almost at the entrance. Fargo flung himself flat as leaden hornets whizzed overhead. He squeezed off two rapid shots, the Colt spewing smoke and death. Cored through the heart, the gunman tottered, his arms and legs going limp. Gamely, he attempted to fire one more time. The shot thudded into the floorboards, kicking up slivers of wood. Then the man's knees buckled and he pitched onto his face.

Rising, Fargo reloaded. Where there were three, there might be more. He walked to the prone figure and nudged it with a toe. The man's blank eyes gaped lifelessly. Underneath him, a scarlet pool spread outward.

"See here! What's the meaning of this?" The desk clerk came around the counter and gawked. "Gunfights are against hotel rules."

"If you hadn't dozed off, none of this would have happened," Fargo gruffly responded. The three assassins had obviously snuck past the clerk while he dozed.

Fargo hastened up to the second floor. All along the hall, doors were opening and worried faces peered out. Squatting beside the first man he'd shot, Fargo rummaged through his pockets. He found a wad of tobacco, a few coins, and fifty dollars in bills, but no clue to the man's identity. Though he badly needed the funds, Fargo couldn't rob a dead man—even one that had been aiming to kill him. In the second gunman's pockets he found another fifty in bills along with a torn slip of paper on which a name and a time had been crudely scrawled: "Harrison's. Ten o'clock."

Did it refer to Charley Harrison, the crime boss of Denver, Fargo speculated? Byers's arch enemy and Ike Talbot's boss? Had Harrison or Talbot or both sent the three killers? Not that it mattered. Fargo didn't take kindly to attempts on his life.

Excited, upset people were spilling from their rooms, some in heavy robes, some in gowns, one man in long underwear. They besieged Fargo with questions, all of them talking at once, demanding to know what had happened.

Ignoring them, Fargo went into his room, over to the closet. He placed the Henry and his saddlebags on the bed, then took a box of cartridges from the saddlebags. Sitting, he loaded the rifle by working the thumb lug to depress the spring and sliding fifteen .44 bullets down the tubular magazine under the barrel. Securing the lug, he worked the lever to feed a cartridge into the chamber.

Fargo pulled on his boots and sat with his back against the headrest, waiting for the inevitable knock. It wasn't ten minutes before an authoritative pounding rocked the door's hinges. "It's open, Marshal."

Denver's answer to law and order was a tall, lanky bundle of sinew and rawhide with features that reminded Fargo of an old hound dog. The lawman's eyes, though, gleamed with keen intelligence as they roved over the Henry in Fargo's lap and then around the room.

Keeping his back to the wall, the lawman entered. He was no greenhorn. In a high holster on his right hip was a Merwin and Hulbert .38 revolver with ivory grips. "Tom Hendly," he said.

Fargo didn't bother introducing himself. He imagined Hendly already knew who he was. "They were sent to kill me."

"I gathered as much."

"Do you know who they were?"

"The one in the flannel was Rufus Carter, a no-account Tennessean. Strayed in here about a year ago and took up with Harrison's crowd." Hendly started to say more but people were poking their heads in the door for a look-see and murmuring like biddies at a Sunday social. "Go back to bed, all of you," he said brusquely. "Everything is well in hand."

The man in the longjohns lingered. "This is an outrage, Marshal! Stray bullets might well have claimed innocent lives! I insist that you arrest this man. I will personally come by your office in the morning to press charges."

Tom Hendly was not one to suffer fools. "You will personally get your ass back in your room or I'll throw *you* behind bars for interfering with an officer of the law in the performance of his official duties."

"You wouldn't!" the man exclaimed.

"Care to try me?" Hendly challenged, and slammed the door in the man's face. "Now then," he said, leaning against the dresser, "I know who you are. Bill Byers stopped by to see me a couple of hours ago. He told me about the palaver you had."

Fargo was curious. "You don't mind having hooded vigilantes roam the streets at night, hanging anyone they feel like it?"

"What do you take me for? Of course I mind. But there's only so much I can do. I'm only one man. The city council hasn't seen fit to hire deputies yet. So I do the best I can." Hendly gazed out the window. "Besides, the vigilantes aren't a bunch of drunken rowdies. They're one hundred of the best citizens this city has to offer. If I bucked them, they'd fire me and hire another lawman. What good would that do?"

"You sound like a man walking a tightrope," Fargo softened.

"Mister, you don't know the half of it." Hendly removed his brown hat and ran a hand through his dark hair. "Sometimes I ask myself why I bother. Why I don't just pack up and ride out before all hell breaks loose. But I've never run from anything in my life and I'm not about to start." He tapped the badge pinned to his vest. "I took an oath when I put this tin on and I mean to keep it, no matter what."

Fargo's respect for the lawman climbed. "Did Byers tell you about the trouble I had with Ike Talbot?"

"Some. Now I'd like to hear it all."

Obliging, Fargo left nothing out. When he was done the lawman jammed his hat back on and curled his hand around his pistol's ivory grips.

"Talbot!" Hendly spat the name venomously. "The worst of the lot, next to Harrison himself. If it weren't against my principles, I'd have put a bullet in his back long ago." He looked at Fargo. "If Talbot's out to get you, he won't stop until he does."

"I'm not about to let him."

The lawman adopted a poker face, a sure sign of secret intent. "Normally, I'd ask you to leave town to avoid bloodshed. But in your case I'll make an exception. You're welcome to stay in Denver as long as you like."

"Why do I rate special treatment?"

Hendly rested an elbow on the dresser. "I'll be honest with you, mister, and lay all my cards on the table." He paused. "As you damn well can see, I'm caught between a rock and a hard place. Between Byers and our illustrious city fathers on one hand, and Harrison and his scum on the other. Two rival fac-

57

tions, ready to go to war if provoked too far. And I'm stuck in the middle, trying my best to keep the violence from getting out of hand."

Fargo thought it strange the lawman would unburden himself to a total stranger. Hendly had an ulterior motive, and Fargo had a hunch what it was.

"I've run scores of Harrison's men out of the city, but new vultures flock in every week to replace them. I've hauled dozens into court only to have the charges thrown out on ridiculous technicalities." Hendly colored with resentment. "I suspect half the judges in Denver are in Harrison's back pocket. The same with many of the politicians, even some of the Committee. He's like one of those octopuses, with his tentacles into everything."

Fargo waited while the marshal chewed on his lower lip.

"I've heard about you. Word is that you have a wild streak but you're not a lawbreaker by nature. You're not a cold-blooded killer. But as you've just proved, you'll throw lead to protect yourself, and when you do, you generally hit what you throw it at."

"And the point of all this?"

"I'm not running you out because I'm hoping you'll do what I can't. I'm hoping you'll gun down Ike Talbot and anyone else who comes at you."

So there it was, as plain as day. "I don't much like being set up as a target in a shooting gallery," Fargo mentioned.

"No one does. But if I'm any judge of character, and I flatter myself that I am, you're not the kind to tuck your tail between your legs and go scurrying off into the hills to avoid a showdown. You'll do what I would do in your boots, namely, hunt Talbot down and end it. Permanently."

Fargo had to hand it to the lawman. Hendly had him figured perfectly. It sparked a troubling thought. "Was this all your idea? Or did William Byers have a hand in it?"

The marshal chuckled. "You're a sharp one, aren't you? Let's just say that Mr. Byers presented a possible scenario, to use his own words, and asked me not to interfere with you in any way."

"I'll be damned," Fargo said. It explained why Byers hadn't lifted a finger against him after he had punched the journalist, and why the vigilantes had been content to leave him alone. His notoriety as a scout and plainsman had little to do with it. Byers wanted to use him to get at Harrison.

"Mr. Byers is mighty shrewd," Tom Hendly said, as if privy to Fargo's thoughts. "He's worked hard to build this city up, so you can't blame him for wanting to guarantee it has a future. It's rough on the man, knowing Denver's fate is in his hands."

"Don't you think he goes a little too far?"

"A little. Sometimes. But balance that in the scales against all the blood Harrison's crowd has spilled, all the innocent folks they've murdered and robbed and cheated, and Mr. Byers is downright saintly in comparison."

Hendly folded his arms across his chest. "You might not have heard, but less than a month ago there was an attempt on Byers's life. Harrison sent four thugs to the *Rocky Mountain News* to kill Byers and destroy the press. But Bill had a shotgun handy. He wounded one, and the others pinned him down. If I hadn't heard the gunfire and come on the run, he wouldn't be alive right now."

Out in the hall someone was yelling, something about dragging the bodies out before they stank up the place.

"This is a struggle for Denver's survival," Hendly said. "It's good pitted against evil, the rule of law against the lawless. You can't blame Byers or me for using every tool at our disposal."

"Including me," Fargo said dryly.

The lawman stepped to the door. "No one is forcing you to do anything. Whether you tangle with Talbot is entirely up to you. You're free to ride on out if you want, with our blessing." So saying, he departed.

Fargo sat and thought for quite some time. The marshal wasn't the only one caught between a rock and a hard place. So was he. Thanks to his lack of funds, he couldn't leave Denver even if he wanted to.

Fargo turned in along about two in the morning, after bolting and locking the door and pushing the dresser in front of it, then pulling down the shade. Unless the cutthroats set the hotel on fire, he would be safe enough for the time being.

The commotion in the corridor had long

since died out. All was still. Fargo lay in bed fully clothed, the Henry at his side. He slept fitfully, awakening whenever he imagined hearing the slightest noise.

Most mornings, Fargo would be up at the crack of dawn. But deep sleep didn't claim him until shortly before five, and it was the middle of the morning before he awakened. Another noise brought him around. Not a faint one like before, but a steady rap on his door. Sitting up and shaking his head to clear lingering cobwebs, he hollered, "Who's there?"

"Mr. Fargo? Skye Fargo? Might I speak with you a moment?"

The voice was a woman's. It wasn't Rosie, and it didn't sound like Delicia. Fargo rose and shoved the dresser back, then opened the door. "Yes?"

A stunning raven-haired beauty in a sky blue dress studied him from the crown of his tousled hair down to the tips of his scuffed boots. She didn't seem particularly impressed. As her gaze lingered on his rumpled buckskins in blatant disdain, she asked, "Are you Skye Fargo? The scout and guide my father told me about?"

Fargo self-consciously smoothed his shirt. "Your father?"

"Professor Rupert T. Cadwell. He and my sister spoke very highly of you." The woman's tone hinted she didn't share their high estimation. "I'm Amity Cadwell, and I have a business proposition for you."

"Business?" Fargo moved back so she could enter. She did so, but cautiously, as if she were walking into a lion's den.

"Do you make it a habit to repeat everything someone says?"

Yawning, Fargo shook himself. "Sorry. Not enough sleep. Now what can I do for you?" Sinking onto the edge of the bed, he noted the ample swell of her bosom and the sweet fragrance that wafted from her skin. She was every bit as lovely as her younger sister but much more serious in her bearing and demeanor.

Amity got straight to the point. "I handle all financial and business matters for our family. As you may have noticed, my father can be quite flighty at times. And my sister, well, let's just say that if she devoted half as much attention to her bank account as she did to her appearance, she would be a millionaire."

"Nicely put," Fargo complimented her.

"By the process of elimination, taking care of our monetary matters is solely up to me. And I'm here now to offer you the sum of three hundred dollars for a week's work. If that's agreeable, of course."

"Three hundred?" Fargo almost leaped up and kissed her. He could pay off the hotel bill and the stable bill and would have enough left over to get him to wherever he wandered to next.

"There you go again," Amity said, "repeating what I say."

"What is it you want me to do?"

"To act as our guide. My father wants to explore the nearby mountains, and he's led me to believe you are quite knowledgeable in that regard. We shouldn't be gone more than a week, perhaps a week and a half."

62

Fargo couldn't help himself. "We?"

Amity sighed loudly. "My sister and I are going along, naturally. We'll provide you with sufficient funds to cover our provisions and to rent mounts."

"It could be dangerous," Fargo said. What with grizzlies and hostiles and badmen, the high country was no place for women. Unless they were women who knew how to ride and shoot.

"Too dangerous for two delicate females, you mean?" Amity was offended. "Don't fret on that score. My sister and I are quite able to take care of ourselves, thank you very much. And we're not about to let our father go traipsing around up there without us." She stared at him, and when he didn't say anything, asked in exasperation, "Well? Do we have an agreement or not, Mr. Fargo?"

"Call me Skye."

"I'll do no such thing. Do you accept my terms? If you're unavailable, I'm sure we can find someone else to guide us. This city is positively crawling with unkempt frontiersmen like yourself."

"We have a deal. I'll take half now, and half when we get back."

"Half?" Amity balked.

"Now who's repeating what the other says?" Fargo repaid her barbs. "One hundred and fifty up front. Plus money for the horses and supplies. I'll get started right away. How soon do you want to leave?"

"How soon can we?"

"Tomorrow morning, bright and early. If

that's all right with you and your father." Fargo grinned when she turned her back to him, opened her bag, and took out her money. She didn't want him to see exactly how much she had. Evidently, she didn't trust him any farther than she could toss him.

"How much will it take to cover our expenses?" Amity inquired.

"Figure two dollars a day for each horse. We'll need three horses to ride, two to use as pack animals. For ten days that's an even hundred. Another fifty for flour, coffee, and other sundries. That should about cover us for now."

Amity handed Fargo money but as he went to accept it, she held on to the bills. "It goes without saying that if you abscond with this, I'll see to it you are hounded to the ends of the earth."

"What do you think I am?" Fargo asked, miffed.

"That remains to be seen. My father asked around about you, and he's under the impression you're a man of impeccable character. To be blunt, I'm more than a little skeptical. If you're the best the West has to offer, I'd say it's a miracle anyone lives west of the Mississippi."

There were only so many insults Fargo would abide. Standing, he jerked the money from her grasp and stuffed it into a pocket. "Act as high and mighty as you want. Just remember—when you walk around with your nose in the air, you never see what you're stepping in."

Amity's jaw muscles twitched. "You're not much of a gentleman, are you?"

"And you're not much of a lady."

In a swirl of blue dress and flowing black hair, Amity Cadwell walked out. Why she didn't demand her money back and tell him to take a short walk off a steep mesa, Fargo couldn't say. Closing the door, he said to the four walls, "Well, that went well." Then he tidied up, washing with water from the basin.

The rest of the day was spent preparing for their trek. The stable owner was all too happy to rent them horses but they had to pay extra for the saddles. Their provisions cost more than Fargo had estimated also, in large part because the influx of gold seekers had driven up the prices.

It was the shank of the evening when Fargo wended his way to the Long's Peak. A note had been left at the front desk. He was to meet the Cadwells in front of the Grand at six the next morning. It gave him the whole night to himself and Fargo knew just what he wanted to do. Rosie O'Grady had mentioned she worked at The House of Mirrors, and now that he had money to spare, he decided to pay her a visit.

Fargo had walked about two blocks when a strange feeling came over him, a feeling he had experienced many times in the wild; the sensation of being watched. He stopped in front of a tailor's and pretended to be interested in the suits on display, but what really merited his interest was the reflection of two men a few dozen yards behind him who had stopped when he did, shifting toward the traffic so he couldn't see their faces. But he wasn't fooled. They were following him.

Fargo walked on, taking his sweet time, checking the reflections of his shadows now and again. They made no attempt to narrow the gap—not yet, anyway—so it was possible their job was merely to trail him and see where he went. He put them to the test at the next side street.

Turning right, Fargo jogged fifty feet to a recessed doorway in a four-story brick building. Ducking into it, he waited, and it wasn't long before the two toughs came hurrying by. They thought he was somewhere ahead; neither glanced into the doorway. As they passed, Fargo stepped out, his right arm at his side. "Looking for someone?"

Their expressions when they spun round were almost comical. Both were in need of a shave and a bath, to say nothing of their greasy, stained clothes. With their narrow, bony faces and lean frames, they resembled nothing so much as a pair of human rats.

"I asked if you were looking for someone?" Fargo prompted when neither of them answered.

The greasier of the pair twitched as if pricked by a pin. "We don't have the slightest idea what you're talkin' about, friend."

"That's right," said the other. "We're just walking along minding our own business. You'd be smart to do the same."

"I thought maybe you were following me," Fargo said. He made no move to draw or to do anything that would spur them into going for their guns.

The nervous one twitched again. "Why in hell would we do that? We don't know you. Never set eyes on you before."

"You must be drunk," the other said.

They backed off, turned, and walked to the end of the block, looking back as they rounded the corner. Fargo mentally counted to ten, then walked to the junction. The pair were hastening eastward. Since he had caught them, they saw no reason to keep dogging his steps. Now, with any luck, they were on their way to report to whomever had sent them.

The shadows lengthened as the sun relinquished the heavens to sparkling stars and a silvery sliver of moon.

Fargo didn't make the same mistake they had. He stayed well back, always a block or more, and always close to buildings so he could duck out of sight if they turned around. Amazingly, they never did. Joking and laughing, they strolled along as if they didn't have a care in the world.

Their meandering route brought them to the red-light district, the area which included notorious Holladay Street. They passed the Cricket Club, for which a more apt name would be the Crooked Club, and the den of wickedness known as the Progressive Club. Their destination turned out to be the Criterion Saloon.

The name jarred Fargo's memory but he couldn't recall why it should. A minute after the pair pushed through the double doors, so did he. His plan was to stay in the shadows and spy on them. But he had hardly taken four steps into the saloon when he saw the pair right in front of him.

With them was Ike Talbot.

5

The Criterion Saloon was packed with patrons. They were four deep at the bar and filled every square foot of space between the gaming tables. The hubbub of voices was so loud that anyone who wanted to make himself heard had to talk twice as loud as they normally would. On a small stage to the left of the bar several skimpily clad ladies danced to the tinny tune of a piano being pounded with vigor by an overweight musician, who had more enthusiasm than talent. Cigar and cigarette smoke hung in a thick cloud below the bar's massive overhead beams.

Skye Fargo angled to the right to lose himself in the swirl of activity before Ike Talbot spotted him, but he didn't succeed. Talbot was facing the entrance and caught sight of him immediately. Fargo's hand fell to his Colt in expectation of having to use it, but Talbot made no move to draw the new Remington on his hip. Smirking, instead the cutthroat swaggered toward him, his two cronies tagging along.

"Well, well, well. And who says prayers aren't answered?"

"I could say the same," Fargo responded. He hoped Talbot would give him an excuse to put an end to the killer's murderous career.

Talbot glanced at the pair who had been shadowing Fargo. "So he never caught on to what you were up to? Isn't that what you just told me? That you'd tricked him? Given him the slip?"

The one with the nervous twitch shrugged. "We thought we had, Ike. Honest to God. He must be smarter than we reckoned."

"Or it could be you're both dumber than you reckon," Talbot said sarcastically. "I guess it's my own fault. Should have sent someone with brains. But I figured the job was so simple, even you two could handle it." He gestured. "Get out of my sight. You'll be docked a day's pay for fouling up. And one more mistake like this, you can look for work elsewhere."

"But, Ike," the nervous one said, "it wasn't our fault. We did exactly as we were told. It isn't fair to hold back our pay."

"Isn't it?"

The question was posed by a large man who had materialized out of the crowd as if out of thin air. He wore a dark suit and a hat almost the same shade as his bushy black beard. A hooked, predatory nose over a slit of a mouth, and glittering dark eyes, lent the impression that just under the surface lurked simmering violence.

"Boss!" the nervous thug declared. "We didn't see you there!"

Fargo gave the man a closer scrutiny. So this was Charley Harrison, the most feared denizen of Denver, the crime lord supposedly responsible for over a dozen grisly deaths, the man who was single-handedly opposing the city fathers for control of their city.

Harrison approached with measured, ponderous steps. "You should learn to be more observant, Gill. Always be aware of what is going on around you. You'll live longer, and be able to do the jobs we ask you to do without botching them."

Gill blanched. He looked as if he couldn't make up his mind whether to faint or take flight. "Please, boss. Please."

"Please what?" Harrison said.

"Don't be mad. We did the best we could. This fella was just too tricky for us, is all. Give Ben and me another job. We'll show you that we can be depended on."

Charley Harrison's hands clenched and unclenched. For a moment Fargo thought he would pounce on the pair, but Harrison hadn't risen to the pinnacle of underworld society by indulging in public displays of violent temper. "Perhaps I will put you to the test. For now, do as Ike advised and make yourselves scarce."

The pair skittered off like frightened rabbits.

Harrison fixed his glittering gaze on Fargo. "So you're the one I've been hearing so much about? We need to have a private talk. Come with me." Without waiting for a reply, Harrison plowed into the throng, making toward a door on the far side.

Fargo didn't like being treated as if he were one of the man's flunkies, but he went along anyway. He noticed how the patrons scurried out of the larger man's path as if out of the path of a prowling grizzly.

In front of the door stood a scarecrow in cheap store-bought clothes, wearing two pistols strapped low. He opened it to admit them.

"No one is to disturb us, Hank. Is that clear?" Harrison said.

"Yes, sir."

The room was lavishly furnished. Plush carpeting, polished furniture, even a small chandelier rivaled the luxuries to be found in any mansion. Harrison walked to a bar and selected a bottle of fine whiskey. "Care for a drink?"

Fargo saw no reason why he shouldn't. He nodded.

"I'll take one too, boss," Ike Talbot said.

Charley Harrison rotated. "My memory must be slipping. I don't recall asking you to join us. Or do you just do whatever you feel like doing nowadays?"

Talbot displayed the same fear Gill had. "I just thought—"

"No, Ike, you don't think," Harrison said with the air of a parent admonishing a wayward child. "Left on your own, you wouldn't last six months. Were it not for me, you'd have long since been thrown into prison or

71

invited to be the guest of honor at a stran-gulation jig officially decreed by the courts."

Talbot backed out. "Say no more. I'll be at the bar if you need me."

"I won't."

Only after the door closed did Harrison indi-cate a chair. "Have a seat. This won't take up much of your time. We need to get a few things straight."

Again the man's imperious air grated on Fargo, but he did as he was bid. The whiskey he was handed was one of the best brands money could buy. It went down as smooth as silk.

"Now then," Harrison said, sinking into a chair across from him, "you're probably won-dering why you weren't gunned down the minute you stepped into my saloon."

"The thought did cross my mind."

"Then know this. I have made it clear to Ike that no one in my organization is to lay a finger on you. If they do, they'll answer to me."

"Why so considerate? Have you taken up religion?"

Harrison's laugh was more like the numbing growl of a silvertip. "I guess you've heard that I don't hesitate to spill blood when it suits my purpose. So obviously killing you doesn't serve any."

"You like to kill, do you?"

"I don't *like* to. I do so when I *have* to. There's a difference." Upending his glass, Har-rison polished off his whiskey in several gulps, then set the glass down on a table with a loud thunk. "Let's quit sparring. I'll lay my cards on the table and you can do the same."

Fargo recalled that the marshal had used the exact same words. "I'm listening."

"First off, I know who are you. I know you're making quite a name for yourself, that you're a crack shot, that you've lived with Indians and can track anything or anyone, anywhere, anytime. I know about the work you've done for the army, and about some of the stories written about you."

"I've heard a lot about you, too," Fargo said.

"None of it any good, if you've heard it from Byers and Hendly. And yes, I know you've met with them. Byers told you that unless I'm put under, Denver will wither and be blown away with the dust. And our illustrious marshal wants to use you to do what he lacks the grit to do himself." Harrison paused. "How am I doing so far?"

Fargo realized the lawman had been right about the crime lord having tentacles everywhere. The only way Harrison could have learned about his talks with Byers and Hendly was if Harrison had spies close to both men. Charley Harrison was indeed a person to be reckoned with.

"Your turn."

"There's not much to tell," Fargo said. "The city fathers blame you for over fifteen murders and want you out of their hair. It's that simple."

"Life is never as simple as some make it out to be," Harrison said. "Take those murders, for instance. The last one was a drunken blacksmith who threatened to split my skull if I didn't let him sit in on a poker game. Sure, he didn't have a gun. But his fists were the size of anvils. I wasn't about to let him pound me into the floor."

Fargo found it peculiar that the most feared man in Denver was trying to justify the reputation he had earned. "What does any of this have to do with me?"

"I just want to make it plain that there are two sides to every story. William Byers called me the Devil Incarnate, didn't he? Yet what makes me so terrible? You've been around, I hear. Traveled all over the place. Compare Denver to, say, San Francisco. There are men there who make me look like a parson by comparison. I'm not the fiend Byers and Hendly painted me as."

Such would seem to be the case, but Fargo couldn't say whether Harrison was sincere or lying through his beard. "Get to the point."

"I'm not out to get you. Talbot tangled with you on his own account, and he'd damn well better not do it again or I'll rip his heart out." Harrison rose to pour himself another drink. "I harbor no ill will toward you whatsoever. You haven't meddled in my affairs, and I'm not about to meddle in yours. What can be fairer?"

"Who sent the three men who tried to kill me at my hotel last night?"

Harrison opened the bottle. "It wasn't me. I only learned about it this morning, along with news of your chats with Byers and the marshal. That's when I called Ike into my office and chewed him out." Leaning against the bar,

Harrison was thoughtful for a moment. "I've risen as high as I have by not overstepping myself, and by not getting carried away with the power I wield. To murder someone as famous as you would cause me no end of grief. Newspapers from coast to coast would carry the story, and maybe some of your friends would come gunning for me. Or the city fathers would use it as an excuse to string me up without a trial, proof or no proof. No, I'm better off leaving you be. And I will—unless you start something first."

Fargo hadn't expected the man to be so reasonable. Granted, Harrison was a sidewinder, but he didn't seem to be the vicious brute others claimed. Rather, he preferred to settle disputes by talking them over rather than resorting to bloodshed. Which gave Fargo the notion that, like Marshal Tom Hendly and William Byers, Harrison had a hidden motive. "What it boils down to is that you're at the top of the heap and you want to stay there. You don't want anyone to do anything that will topple you from your roost."

"That's the situation in a nutshell," Harrison admitted. "Look around you. I live like a king. I make more money in one month than most men earn in a year. I have all the liquor I can want, my pick of the friskiest females anywhere. I'd have to be plumb loco to risk losing all this."

"Then why did you try to have Byers murdered?"

For the first time Charley Harrison showed intense emotion. Pounding the bottle on the bar, he rasped, "I *didn't*! Oh, I sent some men to bust up his office. But only after he waltzed in here and threatened to run daily editorials about my sinful ways, urging everyone to run me out of town."

Fargo didn't know who to believe. Harrison was no angel but neither were the members of the Committee of Safety. According to Rosie, the vigilantes had strung up more men than Harrison had ever killed, and some may have not deserved their awful fate.

"What will it be? Are we enemies or friends?"

Rising, Fargo finished off his drink. "We can never be friends. But so long as you don't try to bury me, I won't come after you."

Harrison grinned. "That's all I ask."

Fargo moved to the doorway. "One last thing. Tell Talbot I don't like being followed."

"That was my doing. Thanks to Ike, word got around yesterday that you were fair game. This morning I told him to let everyone know you're off limits, but I couldn't be sure the message would spread fast enough. So I had him send Gill and Ben to watch your back." Harrison took a swig straight from the bottle. "From here on, though, you can watch your own. See you around."

Not if Fargo could help it. He made a bee-line for the entrance. It was still early and he would look up Rosie. But halfway across the room his name was hollered.

Harrison's lieutenant Ike Talbot, pushed through spectators at a faro table. "What's your secret, mister?"

"Regular baths. You should give it a try."

Talbot wedged his thumbs in his gunbelt, setting into what seemed to be his favorite stance. "What is it between you and the boss? Why is he so all-fired determined not to let you come to harm? What makes you so damn special?"

"Ask him."

"I did, but he wouldn't say." Talbot lowered his voice. "I don't like it. I don't like it one bit. I owe you. And Harrison or no Harrison, I mean to make you pay." A sly grin creased his lips. "Of course, I'll deny I ever said that if you tell Charley."

"Scared of him, are you?"

"I'm not scared of anyone," Talbot boasted, but he didn't raise his voice high enough to be overheard. "Not him. Nor you. As you'll find out before too long."

Fargo was tired of the man's threats and posturing. "Why wait? We'll settle it now. Go for your gun."

Talbot cocked his head. "What?"

"You heard me. Go for your revolver."

"Here? Now?" Talbot laughed, but it was strained, laced with disbelief and a little fear. "The boss would have me skinned alive. He doesn't allow gunplay in the Criterion."

"Convenient excuse, isn't it?" Fargo said, and showing his back to the incensed hardcase, he walked out. The brisk air was invigorating after the smoky, stifling saloon, and he paused to breathe it deep into his lungs.

Bending his steps toward the House of Mirrors, Fargo checked repeatedly over his shoulder but no one was trailing him.

A seething river of humanity frothed along the streets, mainly men eager for feminine companionship and women eager to line their purses. A legion of painted ladies roamed the boardwalks, giving everything in pants a calculated, hungry look. Fargo was propositioned ten times in half as many blocks. He had just declined a bold offer from a dove in a dress three sizes too small and had walked on around the next corner when he nearly bumped into three people walking arm in arm.

"Mr. Fargo! As I live and breathe!"

Professor Rupert T. Cadwell beamed happily at their chance meeting. Delicia's rosy lips parted in a welcoming smile, but Amity Cadwell frowned.

"This is a pleasant surprise," the professor said.

"Speak for yourself, Father," Amity declared.

The professor paid her no mind. "We were tired of being cooped up in our hotel room and came out for a stroll. How stimulating this fair city is! I feel as if I were a robust young man, in the prime of life!"

Fargo wondered if the city was the cause, or the overabundance of underclad women. "This isn't the safest part of Denver to be in after dark," he

"Afraid for us delicate females again?" Amity said.

Delicia let go of her father to link her arm with Fargo's. "Join us, why don't you? We're too excited over our trip into the mountains to turn in early."

"What exactly are you searching for up there?" Fargo asked.

"Geologic formations, my boy," Rupert said. "Conditions and strata only a trained gemologist like myself would recognize."

Delicia gave Fargo a tug. "Let's not talk about silly old rocks and the like. Do you know of a place where we can enjoy some wine in peace and quiet?"

As a matter of fact, Fargo did. The Cork and Spoon served spirits and food, and that was all. The owner, an old whaling man out of Nantucket, didn't peddle in flesh or have dancing girls or gaming tables. But his establishment was tremendously popular. To get there, Fargo had to steer his charges through the worst section of the city, four square blocks where the doves were more bold than ever and every shadowed nook hid potential trouble.

Two of the blocks were behind them when danger brewed.

Fargo had made it a point to walk close to the street to avoid the steady flow of people going into and coming out of the saloons, bars, and illicit houses. But as they were going by a bar, five men barreled out, loud and rowdy and drunk. The foremost was looking over his shoulder when he bumped into Delicia.

"Watch where you're—" the man snapped before swinging around. At the sight of her, he transformed to stone.

"I believe you collided with me, not the other way around," Delicia said cheerfully. "But no harm was done."

"God Almighty!" the man said. "I've died

and gone to heaven! Lookee here, boys! Two visions of loveliness!" The other four pressed in close as he grasped Delicia's hand and pressed it to his lips in an awkward imitation of a titled gentleman. "Twenty dollars for an hour of your time, dearie. How would that be?"

"Oh," Delicia said. "I'm afraid I'm not what you think."

The drunk appraised her like a jeweler appraising a rare gem. "Not cheap, you mean? Then how about forty dollars? That's top rate."

Professor Cadwell put a pudgy hand on the man's sleeve. "You misunderstand, sir. These are my daughters, not ladies of the night. You'll have to find your entertainment elsewhere."

"Sure they're your daughters," the drunk scoffed with an exaggerated wink. "Hell, you can claim she's your mother, for all I care. But forty dollars is all I'm paying." He grabbed Delicia's wrist. "Let's go, honey. There's a boardinghouse down the street where they rent rooms by the hour."

"But I'm not—" Delicia tried to protest, only to be roughly pulled.

Taking a bound, Fargo tore the man's hand off her. "Enough," he warned. "She was telling the truth. There are plenty of other women who will take you up on your offer."

The drunk bristled like a rabid dog. "Did you hear him, boys?" he asked his friends. "This bastard wants to hog her all to himself."

"Not very neighborly of him," one commented.

"It's downright selfish," said another. "And I hate selfish people."

The man who had started the dispute balled his fists. "What say we teach this uppity son of a bitch a lesson?"

Before Fargo could say a thing, they were on him, all five flailing wildly, beating him about his head, shoulders, and chest. In their inebriated state they jostled one another so hard that few of their blows landed solidly, but enough did to drive Fargo to his knees. Only for a moment, however. Girding himself, he surged upward, his own blows precise and direct. His knuckles slammed into a jutting chin, into a protruding paunch, and into the face of another. Three were down, cursing and groaning, in twice as many seconds.

The remaining pair weren't to be denied. Lowering their shoulders, they tackled Fargo, their combined weight enough to smash him flat into his back. He kneed one in the groin, but the other, a hefty bruiser with fingers as thick as railroad spikes, wrapped his hands around Fargo's throat to throttle the life out of him.

"Damn you, you bastard!" the man railed.

Fargo sought to pry his fingers from his neck but each was like an iron vise, and growing tighter by the second. They gouged into his windpipe, cutting off his breath. He battered the man's ears but it had the same effect as punching a tree stump.

Suddenly a twin-barreled derringer was pressed against the bruiser's temple. "That will be quite enough," Amity Cadwell said.

"We need him to serve as our guide or I'd gladly let you throttle him."

Befuddled by the booze, the bruiser glanced up. But his grip didn't slacken. "Who are you tryin' to bluff, lady? You're a woman. Women don't shoot people."

"Do they kick them?" Amity asked, and did exactly that, planting her shoe squarely in the center of his broad face.

Cartilage crunched. The drunken bruiser howled like a stricken coyote, raised up onto his knees, and covered his ruptured, spurting nostrils. "You bitch!" he bawled. "You broke my nose!"

Amity cocked the derringer. "That's not all I'll do if you ever insult me like that again."

The drunk believed her. Cowering, he slid backward. His friends were sitting up now, except for the one Fargo had kneed.

"We're not whores, you pathetic cretins," Amity informed them. "Were any of you able to think straight, you'd realize that fact." She sidestepped past them. "Father. Delicia. And, Mr. Fargo, if you'd be so kind. Let's leave these wretches to their suffering."

Rubbing a sore spot on his shoulder, Fargo moved on down the street. "Thanks for the help," he said.

"I did it for my father, not for you." Amity placed the derringer back into her bag. "I couldn't care less if they had beat you to a pulp."

"You like me that much?"

"I like you that little."

In all his travels Fargo had never met a

woman quite like Amity Cadwell. Her beautiful exterior concealed a heart of stone. She was solid ice through and through. "When was the last time a man asked you out?"

Amity glanced up. "What the hell does that have to do with anything? Are you implying that because I'm not a giddy weakling like most women, I'm somehow less desirable to the opposite sex?"

"I couldn't have said it better myself."

"You overstep your bounds, mister. My personal life is none of your business. Never bring it up again."

"Or what? You'll shoot me?"

Amity started to reach into her bag but Professor Cadwell stepped between them. "Please, my dear. Be civil. We must try our best to get along. We don't want to get our expedition off on the wrong foot, now do we?"

"I don't like him," Amity declared.

"Be that as it may, his abilities as a scout are unrivaled. Even more importantly, everyone I've talked to has said he is scrupulously honest. He is exactly what we need."

Fargo didn't understand why his honesty was so important, unless they were worried he'd take the advance money they had given him and ride out without fulfilling his end of their agreement. Taking the lead, he presently spied the Cork and Spoon up ahead. "There's the place we want."

Delicia came alongside him. "Don't let my sister get to you, handsome. She treats everyone the same way she treats you."

"And you put up with it?"

"She wasn't always so mean. The death of our mother years ago changed her something terrible."

Fargo glanced back at the raven-tressed iceberg and the professor. It was well he did. For behind them, approximately half a block, were two familiar figures—Gill and Ben, the pair of gunmen Charley Harrison had sent to keep an eye on him. Harrison had promised not to do it again. Yet there they were. And the instant Fargo laid eyes on them, the two curly wolves stabbed their hands to their hardware and commenced shooting.

6

Skye Fargo shoved a startled Delicia Cadwell to the ground, then dived at her father and sister, tackling both at the same time. The professor squawked in consternation as Fargo bore them hard to the earth.

The crack of six-shooters punctured the ruckus created by passing carriages and passersby. Fargo heard lead whiz by above them as he rolled to the left and drew his Colt. Gill and Ben were blasting away like frenzied lunatics, neither bothering to aim. They didn't come nearer, and didn't press their advantage in any way. Which was fine by Fargo. He banged a shot at Ben, who clutched his shoulder and bawled out that he was hit.

Gill fanned his pistol twice more, then

turned on his heels and shouted, "Let's get out of here! We'll finish it another time!"

The two gunmen sped off into the night.

Pushing upright, Fargo started after them, yelling to the professor, "Head for your hotel!" The Cadwells were sitting up, Rupert and Delicia dumbfounded by the turns of events, Amity appearing more mad than anything else.

Fargo took it for granted that he, not the Cadwells, had been the intended target. The attack mystified him. Charley Harrison had seemed genuinely sincere about not wanting to incite trouble between them. Apparently, though, Harrison had only intended to lull him into letting down his guard so he would be easy to gun down. If Gill and Ben hadn't rashly gone for their hardware, the scheme might have worked.

The pair were running flat out, knocking aside anyone and everyone who didn't get out of their way quick enough to suit them. Ben was in pain, a dark stain marking the back of his shirt, but he was able to keep up with his friend Gill, who was reloading on the fly.

Fargo didn't try to drop them. There were too many innocent bystanders who might take a stray slug. At the next corner the gunmen took a right and Fargo slowed, wary of being ambushed, but a peek around the bend showed the two men still sprinting for all they were worth. They had chosen a less frequented thoroughfare so they could run that much faster.

None of the pedestrians tried to intervene,

which was understandable. Many of Denver's citizens didn't carry firearms. Those who did weren't about to take the law into their own hands and possibly be riddled with bullets for their efforts.

Nor could Fargo count on the marshal for aid. Hendly might be anywhere in the sprawling city. The lawman was sure to investigate the sound of so much gunfire, but by the time he reached the vicinity, it would be too late to be of any help.

Gill and Ben were surprisingly fleet of foot. Fargo realized they might outdistance him unless he summoned all the speed he was capable of. He saw Ben glance back and raise his revolver, and veered wide as it spat smoke and hot death.

Gill barked something at Ben, probably telling him not to waste lead, and Ben faced front, redoubling his efforts.

For another minute their headlong flight continued. A woman screamed when Gill violently shoved her aside. Another pedestrian, was too slow in moving and received a clout to the head that sent him to his knees with blood oozing from a smashed ear. Then an alley mouth loomed, dark and foreboding like the maw of a giant beast, and the two gunmen darted into it.

Fargo slowed again. To do otherwise invited a hail of lead. Crouching, he peered around the corner and saw that the alley extended for a full block. No silhouettes were visible, so Gill and Ben had to be in there somewhere, hiding, waiting for him to blunder into their hastily contrived trap. Large, vague objects dotted the alley, offering plenty of places for them to hide.

Fargo replaced the spent cartridge in his Colt and added a sixth under the hammer. Leaning back, he waited, letting it grate on their strained nerves. He wanted them to be so jumpy that they would squeeze off their first shots without thinking. People stopped to stare but he didn't care. When a young man started toward him as if to ask a question, Fargo waved the man off.

Finally, Fargo moved. He flung himself into the alley on his belly. Flames stabbed the darkness and artificial thunderclaps echoed between the buildings. A slug bit into the dirt near his elbow, another into the wall on his right. Fargo answered in kind, firing twice, then flipped to the left against the base of the other wall.

Fargo swore he could hear his blood pounding in his temples in the deafening silence that ensued. He calmed himself, taking shallow breaths while probing the alley from end to end. He had a fair notion where one of the gunmen was concealed, but not the other. Groping the ground, he found a small stone.

Furtive movement signaled that the pair were up to something. Fargo threw the stone at a spot about ten feet ahead and to the right. It had the desired result. Gill and Ben both cut loose, shooting at the sound. Fargo, in turn, shot at their barrel flashes, twice each, and was rewarded with a loud grunt and a curse.

Again quiet claimed the alley. Fargo quickly reloaded, then snaked forward. Or snailed forward, more like it, an inch at a time, to avoid drawing their fire.

Someone coughed, a gurgling sort of rasp typical of those with a severe lung wound. "I'm hit bad, Gill," Ben whispered. "Skedaddle. I'll hold him off as long as I can."

"I'm not leavin' you, pard."

"I tell you I'm done in. Go. Now. I'm liable to keel over any second."

Their whispers informed Fargo of their approximate positions. He crawled another couple of inches. Suddenly an inky figure materialized and commenced spraying the alley with lead. Fargo responded, seeing the figure jolt backward then disappear behind a crate. Further down another indigo shape sped toward the far street. Fargo raised the Colt but didn't fire. He couldn't bring himself to shoot Gill in the back, even if it was what Gill deserved.

Ben's revolver banged, and a slug thudded into the wall close above Fargo's head. He thumbed off two rapid shots, then slid to the right and lay still.

Gill ran out of the alley and was gone. Fargo vowed they would meet again soon, and the next time neither one of them would live to walk away.

Faint sounds ahead warned Fargo that the other hardcase was still alive. Whether Ben was behind the crate or had moved, Fargo was unsure. With the patience of a hunter he waited for the other man to make the first move.

Time dragged on, as if weighted by mill-stones. After ten or fifteen minutes Fargo began to question the wisdom of waiting any longer. Feeling about him with his left hand, he found a ragged length of planking, which he threw toward the crate. It clattered noisily but there was no reaction.

Swiveling, Fargo kicked the wall. Once more nothing happened. Slowly rising into a crouch, he advanced, placing each boot down with care. He was almost to the crate when he saw a pair of legs jutting out from behind it. Freezing, he watched to see if the legs were moving. They weren't. Bracing himself, he bounded past the crate and leveled the Colt.

Ben was slumped over, his forehead against the crate, his six-shooter on the ground beside him. Tiny sucking sounds came from his chest.

Sinking onto a knee, Fargo flipped the gunman's revolver out of reach. He pressed a finger to the man's neck and felt a feeble pulse. Ben's mouth moved, the words he uttered barely audible.

"What was that? I didn't catch it."

Ben slowly lifted his head high enough to stare Fargo in the face. "You stinking bastard. You've made worm food of me."

Fargo gripped him by the shoulders and pushed him against the wall. "You brought it on yourself. Or the man who sent you did. Who was it?"

"I'll never tell." Ben grinned wickedly, then broke into a fit of convulsive coughing.

When it ended, his chin was lathered with blood and the sucking sounds in his chest were twice as loud.

"Was it Harrison?" Fargo persisted.

Ben looked up. "Means to an end, that's all you are," he said weakly. "Won't live out the week."

"Means to an end?"

"Five hundred," the gunman said in a strangled whisper.

"Five hundred what?"

"Dollars. On your head." Ben tried to laugh but he hacked instead, doubling over, his whole body shaking in tremendous heaves. His fingers clawed at the dirt, then went limp. A few seconds later his entire body followed suit.

Fargo slowly stood. Someone had put a bounty on him? The only likely candidate was Charley Harrison. He turned toward the alley mouth and saw someone framed in the opening. Instinctively, he brought up the Colt.

"It's me, Fargo. Marshal Hendly." The lawman entered and walked up to the crate. He inspected the dead gunman, and frowned. "One of Harrison's outfit. Let me guess—he tried to kill you."

"Him and one other," Fargo absently replied. He was mulling over the implications of the price on his hide.

"I warned you, didn't I?" Hendly said. "What more proof do you need that Harrison is out to get you? I'm surprised you haven't paid him a visit by now."

Fargo moved to the street and holstered his pistol. He related the essentials of the gunfight to the lawman.

"I'll tend to the body," the marshal offered. "But if you want my advice, you'll stay off the streets until daylight. And watch your back at all times."

A crowd was gathering, so Fargo nodded at Hendly and left. Despite Charley Harrison's reputation, he couldn't quite believe the crime boss had sent the assassins. Something told him there was more to it, but exactly what was impossible to say.

The Grand Hotel was Fargo's first stop. At the front desk he aked for the Caldwells' room number. The stuffy desk clerk gave his dusty, smudged buckskins a withering look of disapproval as he started up the stairs.

The professor was in 219, the women in 220. Fargo knocked on Professor Cadwell's door first but there was no response. At the second room, he heard muted conversation which ended with his rap.

Amity opened the door. Her look of disapproval was almost as severe as the clerk's had been. "We've been sitting here debating whether we should hire someone else to be our guide," she curtly announced.

"I'm fine. Thanks for worrying," Fargo said as he strode by her. Professor Cadwell leaped up from a chair to clasp him by the shoulders.

"My friend! You're alive! We feared you had been murdered!" Rupert gave his oldest daughter a severe look. "That's the reason, the *only* reason, we were discussing the possible need to replace you. But I refused to do so until we had heard the outcome."

Delicia had been perched on the bed. Now she surprised Fargo by embracing him and kissing him on the cheek. "Thank goodness you're all right! Who were those two men? Why did they try to kill us?"

"It was me they were after," Fargo revealed. He told them about the price on his head, but not about Charley Harrison or William Byers having any hand in it.

"But who would do such a terrible thing?" Professor Cadwell asked.

"You poor dear," Delicia sympathized, giving Fargo's arm a tender squeeze. "You must be worried sick over when they'll try again."

Amity didn't share their concern. "Will you listen to the two of you? Forget about him. Think about us, and what this means for our trek into the mountains. If someone tries to pick him off, we might wind up caught in the crossfire."

Delicia turned. "How can you be so cruel? Is that all you can think of? How it will effect you?"

"I'm thinking of all us," Amity said gruffly. "We're putting our lives at risk if we let him lead us. I vote we hire someone else."

As much as Fargo hated to admit it, she had a point. They would be in greater peril with him along.

Professor Cadwell raised a hand. "Let's not snip at one another, girls. Reason this out like intelligent, mature adults instead of allowing your emotions to sweep you away." He reclaimed the chair. "Mr. Fargo has been exceptionally frank with us, and I feel it is our responsibility to be just as frank with him." He propped his feet on the night table. "I would be remiss if I didn't confess this latest development worries me. But not nearly as much as being delayed. Need I remind you time is at a premium? We can't afford to squander a single day. So I vote that we continue as planned."

Amity was tremendously displeased. "Have you thought this out, Father?"

"Of course," Professor Cadwell said, sounding slightly offended. "Haven't you? I reiterate. It might take us up to a week or more to find someone as qualified as Fargo. Do you comprehend what a delay of that magnitude means?"

Delicia cut in. "I do. It would ruin everything. So Fargo gets my vote, too. I have every confidence he'll see us safely through."

"Is it confidence or passion that influences you most?" Amity asked.

"Are you implying I'm unduly fond of him?" Delicia retorted, placing her hands on her hips.

Amity didn't hold back. "You're fond of anything in britches. Where other women collect knickknacks, you collect men. If I had a dollar—"

Delicia hiked a fist. Amity promptly curled her fingers into claws. But their father was between them before either could tear into the other. Rupert pushed them apart, none too gently, and frowned.

"Is this any way to behave? Especially in front of our guest? He must think the two of you are about as mature as five-year-olds. Please try to act your ages until our stay in Denver is concluded. Then you can indulge your petty animosities to your hearts' content."

Fargo cleared his throat. "I should have a say in this. And I vote the same as Amity. It's too dangerous for me to lead you. You'll have to find someone else." He assumed that would make Amity happy, and that she'd eagerly agree, but to his utter amazement she did the exact opposite.

"Not so fast. If our father believes it's in our best interest to go with you, then that's what we'll do. We'll be ready to depart at dawn, exactly as we've arranged. Just be sure you're out in front of the hotel with our horses and supplies at the appointed hour."

To say Fargo was perplexed was the understatement of the century. One minute Amity was dead set against having him along, yet in the next she refused to let him back out of their deal. It made no sense whatsoever.

"Then it's settled," Professor Cadwell said gleefully. "Everyone is agreed. In two days we'll be high up in the Rockies. After that, who knows?" He winked at both his daughters. Delicia tittered. Amity merely smiled.

"If you're sure," Fargo said.

"Is there any other news you wanted to share?" Amity inquired. "If not, it's late, and we need to get some sleep. So why don't you do us a favor and leave?"

"Amity!" Delicia protested. "You can be so rude!"

Fargo walked to the door. "That's all right. Some people just can't help making a jackass of themselves."

If glares could kill, Amity's would have reduced Fargo to a pile of smoldering ash. Fargo had never met a woman who disliked him so intensely for so little reason. As he went to leave, Delicia took his hand.

"I'll walk you to the landing. It's the least I can do to make up for my sister's abominable behavior." She glanced at her father. "If that's all right with you?"

"Be my guest, daughter," Professor Cadwell said.

The hallway was deserted. Fargo became supremely aware of the vivacious blonde's lush body and flowing flaxen hair. The warmth of her palm against his started a prickling in his loins. "You don't need to do this," he said.

"Oh, hush." Delicia, grinning, contrived to press her side against his. Speaking softly, she said, "I want you to know how much I'm looking forward to our little adventure. We'll be all alone up in the high country. Just the four of us, that is."

"Have any of you ever been in the Rockies before?"

"No, we sure haven't," Delicia said. Her fingernail rubbed his forefinger. "I'm as thrilled as can be. I can't imagine anything that would make me more excited."

"Even this?" Stopping, Fargo pulled her close and kissed her full on the mouth. His hands cupped her bottom, kneading her posterior as if she were bread dough. Delicia vented a tiny moan, her hips grinding into him. She was incredibly soft, incredibly delicious, and incredibly arousing. At length she stepped back, her cheeks flushed beet red.

"Oh, my. What you do to me." Delicia smiled coyly. "Now I'm looking forward more than ever to our journey. It promises to be more stimulating than I would have thought possible." Winking, she pranced back to the room, the unconsciously seductive sway of her hips causing Fargo to lick his lips in carnal hunger.

The long walk back to his hotel was spent in deep thought.

Fargo had found himself caught in the middle of a bloody war that pittied Denver's criminal underworld against the city fathers. He wanted no part of it, but it seemed that forces he couldn't control were intent on involving him whether he liked it or not.

And as if that were not enough to occupy him, he was about to take three tenderfeet up into the most rugged, most unforgiving, most savage country anywhere.

It just might be that for once, he had bitten off more than he could chew.

Twelve hours later, well up into the Emerald Foothills that flanked Denver to the west, Skye Fargo twisted in the saddle to check on the rest of his party, who were strung out in single file behind him. Professor Cadwell was astride a mare the stable owner had assured Fargo was as gentle as a newborn lamb. Delicia, attired in a recently purchased riding outfit, rode a sorrel sidesaddle. Amity, in a matching outfit, was on a big bay, leading the two packhorses. It had been agreed upon that the Cadwells would take turns handling the pack animals to free Fargo for the more important task of guiding them and keeping his eyes peeled for trouble.

Professor Cadwell, in fine fettle, chittered like a chipmunk. In his estimation the day was "simply spectacular." The air was "giddily intoxicating." The snow-crowned peaks that loomed ahead were "Nature's lavish glory." Rupert had been waxing eloquent about anything and everything for so long, Fargo wished the man would shut up for a while.

As he had done dozens of times since they left the city limits, Fargo scoured their back trail. He saw no riders, no telltale tendrils of dust. He was fairly convinced no one was following them but he wouldn't rest easy until he had brought the three easterners back safe and sound.

"Yes, indeed," the professor started up again. "On magnificent days like these, I'm happy I took up the profession I did. I couldn't stand being chained to a desk ten hours a day, or laboring down in the depths of a mine, or slaving away in a farm field under the burning sun." He gestured. "This is the life! Adventure! The outdoors! What more could a person ask for?"

A little less gabbing, Fargo reflected. But he couldn't very well command Cadwell to keep quiet. And since the professor was being so talkative, Fargo decided it was a good time to find out the man's purpose. "You still haven't told me what it is that you're looking for up here."

"In due course all will be made clear, my friend," Rupert said. "For now, all you need know is that I desire to see some sites above the tree line where a lot of loose rock is present. Talus slopes would do nicely."

Frontiersmen, Fargo among them, routinely fought shy of talus. It was notoriously treacherous, as many an unwary rider had learned to their fatal regret. Horses couldn't keep their footing on the yards-deep layer of loose stone and dirt.

"You can find some for us, can't you?" Cadwell eagerly asked.

"If we ride all day and most of tomorrow, we can be at a large talus slope I know of by tomorrow evening," Fargo predicted. Exactly what it was the professor hoped to find there eluded him.

"Excellent. Most excellent," Rupert said, and gestured at his daughters. "Did you hear that, girls? By tomorrow night!"

"Don't get your hopes up," Amity said. "The geological conditions might not be favorable. We might need to examine several other sites."

"Of course, of course," Professor Cadwell said, "but the prospects are most encouraging. I can't wait to get there."

Onward they forged, always upward, beyond the foothills into the mountains proper. Truth be told, Fargo was happy to be back in the saddle again, glad to be shed of civilization. Towns and cities always lost their appeal after a while, and a craving for the wilderness would inevitably come over him, a desire to be among the free, wild things that roamed to their heart's content, just as he loved to do.

The route Fargo had selected was well off the beaten path. Once they left the rutted excuse for a road that linked Denver to the mining camps, they saw no other travelers. Wildlife was abundant, though. Bald eagles soared high on the currents. Hawks wheeled in search of prey. Deer grazed unafraid in forest and dell. Squirrels, chipmunks, and jays chattered everywhere.

To the northeast towered Long's Peak, the regal mountain Fargo's hotel had been named after. Almost three miles high, a mantle of almost year-round snow lent it regal splendor. A phalanx of lesser peaks thrust skyward on all sides, presenting a formidable natural rampart that until a few short decades ago had seemed to be an impassable barrier preventing westward expansion.

But now hordes of people crossed the Rockies every year. Immigrants bound for the Oregon Country used the gently sloping South Pass. Gold and silver seekers and anyone else who wanted to penetrate deep into the mountains relied on other gaps, some discovered just within the past few years.

Fargo knew most of them, and quite few

other passes no one had ever heard of. He'd learned about them from the Indians, from grizzled old mountain men, and from his own meandering travels. Up near one such high notch was the talus area he had in mind. It was shortly before sunset when he finally saw it way off in the distance, distinguished by a series of rocky cliffs that served as a landmark.

They pitched camp on a high shelf in a clearing in dense pines that would shelter them from the chill night wind. Another reason Fargo chose the spot was the ribbon of a stream that flowed across the shelf. Dismounting, he loosened the Ovaro's cinch, then removed his saddlebags.

"Professor, I want you to fetch water for coffee while I strip and tether the horses. Your daughters can gather firewood." Fargo opened the saddlebags, removed his coffeepot, and turned. Not one of them had moved. "Something wrong?"

Amity answered. "I should say there is. Why do you think we hired you? Common chores are your job, not ours."

"You hired me to be your guide, not your servant," Fargo said. "So either all of you help out or we'll head back to Denver first thing in the morning."

"I don't mind lending a hand," Delicia said, sliding down off of her mount. Her leather skirt slid partway up her legs, revealing a tantalizing glimpse of slender calves and velvet thighs.

"Of course you wouldn't," Amity groused.

Professor Cadwell awkwardly yanked a foot from a stirrup. "Don't grumble. It won't kill you to soil your hands. And the potential rewards are worth the inconvenience."

Fargo tossed the coffeepot to Rupert and tried to ignore their petty bickering. Ultimately, Amity reluctantly gave in, and Rupert trudged off to get water. By then Fargo had removed two of the saddles and saddle blankets and was starting on the third.

In the meantime Delicia had collected an armful of deadwood which she deposited in the middle of the clearing. "This isn't so bad," she told her sister.

"If he asked you to lick his boots, would you do that too?" Amity responded.

Fargo toyed with the idea of leaving them by the fire and sleeping somewhere else. He flipped a stirrup up, then stiffened.

From the direction of the stream rose a piercing wail of mortal terror. "Help me!" Professor Cadwell cried. "God in heaven, someone help me!"

7

Skye Fargo had his Colt out and was crashing through the brush before the echoes of the professor's strident wail faded. He only had twenty yards to cover, and when he emerged from the undergrowth he saw Cadwell over by the stream, a hand pressed to his throat.

Fargo looked both ways but saw nothing to account for the scream. "What is it?"

Rupert's mouth moved but no words came out. Teetering as if about to faint, he hobbled backward, into the arms of Amity and Delicia, who had arrived within seconds.

"What did you see?" Fargo demanded, still scouring the area. He envisioned a hulking grizzly, or maybe painted warriors on the warpath.

"S—s—snake," Cadwell stuttered.

"A snake?"

"Yes. There. In those weeds by the water."

Fargo stepped to the reeds. "What kind of snake? A rattler?" He figured it had to be the biggest anyone had ever seen to spark such raw terror.

"I don't know. It was greenish and had some stripes and a forked tongue."

To Fargo, it sounded like a harmless ribbon snake. "Why did you scream? Did it try to bite you?" Even if it had, their bites were no worse than a strong pinch.

"It looked at me."

"That's all?"

"You should have been here! That dreadful serpent looked right at me with its horrible, slitted eyes and flicked its long tongue. I've never seen a snake in the wilds before, and I was never so petrified in my life. But I couldn't run. My legs wouldn't work. So I did the next best thing."

Pursing his lips in disgust, Fargo headed for the clearing. He was beginning to have grave doubts about the whole venture. If it wasn't for the three hundred dollars—and Delicia—he'd take them back to Denver right that minute.

"Wait!" Rupert said. "Aren't you going to hunt it down and shoot it? I won't feel safe until I see its remains."

"Hell, you scared it as badly as it scared you. By now it's probably halfway down the mountain."

Fargo finished unsaddling their mounts and unloaded the packhorses. He kindled a fire, then set coffee on to boil. Professor Cadwell and the women roosted on a nearby log and were discussing their mysterious enterprise in hushed tones when Fargo yanked the Henry from the saddle scabbard and turned to the pines.

"Where are you going?" the professor inquired.

"We need to eat."

"What will you bring us?" Rupert asked. "Venison, perhaps? I love thick, juicy steaks. Or if not deer meat, how about some succulent elk?"

"Maybe snake meat," was Fargo's parting shot. He hadn't gone far when he heard footfalls hurrying to catch him. He knew who it was before he turned around. "Go back with the others."

Delicia Cadwell arched her finely defined eyebrows. "Whatever for? I was hoping for a little while alone with you."

With her hair spilling over her shoulders like strands of pure gold, her full bosom and finely sculpted hips superbly outlined by the clinging leather outfit, Delicia was as lovely as could be. Fargo reminded himself that sunset wasn't far off and he had to hunt while the light lasted. "I need to move quietly," he lamely explained.

"I can move just as quietly as you can," Delicia said. Coming up to him, she put a hand on his shoulder. "Please. I promise not to be a bother. And Father said it was all right."

Fargo's common sense waged war with a hunger that had no relation to food. His eyes roved over the swell of her large breasts and down to the equally alluring curves of her thighs. "Suit yourself," he said, surrendering to his craving.

Grinning, Delicia idly stroked his jaw. "Thank you, handsome. You won't regret it."

Game on the narrow shelf was scarce. A few squirrels, a few jays, and that was about it. Fargo climbed an adjoining timbered slope, the trees so close together that the forest floor was shrouded in shadow. A carpet of pine needles deadened their footsteps.

Delicia was true to her word. She didn't make much noise. She had the presence of mind to place her feet exactly where Fargo did, walking in his very footsteps. He glanced back at her several times and she always smiled warmly, an unmistakable invitation in the depths of her smoldering eyes.

As a result, Fargo found it hard to concentrate on what he was doing. He saw sparrows, and some chipmunks, and then caught sight of a white-tail doe that bounded off before he could take hasty bead.

Several hundred yards from the campsite Fargo started to loop in a wide circle that would eventually lead them back to the fire. He didn't care to stray too far from the professor and Amity. There was no telling when a grizzly or hostiles might happen by. And while Amity could take care of herself, her father, for all his university degrees, was ridiculously incompetent. Maybe it was because Rupert had spent so much time with his nose buried in books, he hadn't learned how to survive in the real world.

Fargo had met people like Rupert before. One had been a butterfly collector, a naturalist who wouldn't have lasted five minutes in the wilderness on his own. There had been a scientist who came West to study what he'd called the "diversity of montane fauna in its natural habitat," and who thought nothing of crawling down into a rattlesnake den to count how many were there.

People like that mystified Fargo. They seemed to go through life with blinders on, so swept up in their private pursuits they were oblivious to danger. How any of them lived to a ripe old age was an enigma in itself.

A hint of movement to the right brought Fargo to a stop. He scolded himself for letting his thoughts drift as he scoured the underbrush. There it was again. A large rabbit was nibbling on shoots. With its long, sensitive ears, it must have heard them, but it hadn't run off yet. Fargo tucked the Henry's stock to his shoulder.

"You're going to shoot that poor bunny?" Delicia whispered.

"Unless you want to go hungry tonight, yes," Fargo answered, sighting down the barrel.

"But it looks so cute. I'd rather you shot a deer."

"It's almost dark and there are none around," Fargo noted. Then there was the matter of letting all the extra meat go to waste. Between the four of them they could eat a haunch, but over two-thirds of the deer would be left, and Fargo doubted the professor would be willing to stick around for a few days so they could smoke and cure it.

"That poor sweet little thing," Delicia said.

Fargo fired. At the boom of the retort the rabbit leaped high into the air, only to fall onto its side and lie twitching, its legs pumping as if it were running.

"You did it! You really did it!"

"What did you expect?" Fargo looked at her. Delicia's eyes were moist. "There aren't any restaurants up here. We either kill our own food or we starve, and I'm partial to staying alive."

"I know, I know. It's just—" Delicia dabbed at her eyes with a sleeve. "I'm sorry. I'm acting childish. But I had a pet bunny when I was little. It was run over by a grocer's wagon, and I bawled for a month."

Fargo was caught off guard when she pressed her face to his shoulder. He held her, the Henry in his left hand, the feel of her bosom against his chest, and the contact of her thighs provoking notions better left alone. He thought she was going to cry but she stood quietly, her breath warm on his neck.

"Are you all right?" he asked after a bit, his voice huskier than usual.

"Fine," Delicia whispered. She brushed her lips along his neck to his ear, her tongue rimming his earlobe.

"What do you think you're doing?"

"Isn't it obvious?"

Yes, it was, and Fargo could think of a dozen reasons why they shouldn't do what she had in mind but all of them went up like so much dry tinder in a bonfire as her licking and nibbling set his blood to boil. He leaned the Henry against a fir, then lowered his mouth to hers, kissing her hungrily, forcefully, his tongue pushing past her teeth to find her own.

Delicia groaned deep in her throat. She melted against him, her hands reaching up around his neck to lock behind his head. The fragrance of her perfume was as intoxicating as the sensual sensations her lips and hands provoked.

Fargo scanned the vegetation, insuring no nasty surprises lurked there, while his hands drifted down to her bottom and cupped it as he had in the hotel. She ground against him, her legs rubbing against his as if she were seeking to generate enough friction to set his buckskins ablaze.

"You kiss marvelously," Delicia breathed.

Fargo kissed her neck and licked her smooth, delicate throat. She arched her spine, her breasts thrusting against him, her hands running up through his hair and upending his hat.

107

He let it tumble. His tongue lapped at her ear, sending shivers through her luscious body.

"Oh, yes!"

The top half of her leather outfit was easy to part. A few buttons, a hook, and the deed was done. Her undergarments only delayed Fargo a few seconds. Then her glorious mounds spilled out, her nipples two inviting, erect peaks. He sucked on one, then the other, alternating back and forth while squeezing and massaging each breast, slowly but surely stroking Delicia to a feverish carnal pitch.

"Don't stop. Please don't stop!"

Her leather skirt was thicker than a dress. Fargo decided that bunching it around her waist would rumple it and might arouse her father's suspicions. So he opted to remove it, and cast it aside. He did all this while continuing to give her exquisite breasts the attention they merited. Delicia was panting like a blacksmith's bellows, her nails digging into his shoulders, when he ran a hand across her marble thighs and brushed a finger across the entrance to her innermost delights.

"Ahhhhhh!" She quivered, her head thrown back, her mouth open seductively.

Fargo nibbled on her lips, and inhaled her silken tongue. His pole was fully erect and straining for release. As he reached for his belt buckle, a new sensation crept across his skin. A sensation that had nothing to do with lovemaking. A sensation that they were being watched.

Long ago Fargo had learned never to ignore

his intuition. More times than he could recall it had saved his life. So when his skin began to crawl as if a thousand ants covered him, he cracked his eyelids and scoured the timber again. Nothing moved other than a few sparrows. Yet he couldn't shake the feeling.

Instead of lowering Delicia to the carpet of pine needles, he slid around behind her. She glanced quizzically at him, then grinned when he undid his belt to free his imprisoned manhood.

"Oh, my! You're such an animal."

Fargo took that as a compliment. Lowering his right hand, he brushed it across her moist, hot slit. She arced her back, cooing like a lovebird. Finding her tiny knob, he gently flicked and caressed it. At every touch Delicia shook like a leaf in a gale. Throaty moans escaped her, rising in volume.

Inserting a finger, Fargo slowly stroked her. She loved it. Her slick inner walls contracted with every stroke, and she began rubbing her backside on his organ, up and down, up and down, hardening him like iron. When he slid a second finger in and thrust both deeper, Delicia tossed her mane of golden hair like a mare about to be mounted by a stallion.

"Oh! Yes! More! More!"

The sensation of being watched continued to bother Fargo. It was why he had decided to stand up rather than lie down. At least he could keep an eye on the surrounding woodland. Prone, they would be too vulnerable.

"I've wanted you since the moment I laid eyes on you," Delicia husked.

Fargo planted both boots and aligned his member with her womanhood. Rubbing himself across her, he caused her to groan long and loud. He reached around, held her securely by the waist, tensed his leg muscles, and speared up into her with all his might.

Delicia's head snapped back, her lovely eyes wide. For several seconds she was perfectly still, then she began to move against him, into him, burying him deeper inside. Her satiny inner core sheathed him like a velvet glove.

For his part, Fargo cupped both her breasts to give himself the leverage he needed. Tweaking and squeezing them, he rocked his hips back and forth. Slowly at first, with rising urgency, he drove himself up into her.

All the while, the sensation of being watched pricked Fargo like a thousand pins. He continually scanned the brush, hoping it wasn't a grizzly. The bear would be on them before he could grab the Henry. But the same intuition that told him he was being spied on made him think it wasn't a silvertip. It was something else.

Or, rather, *someone* else.

Waves of delight rippled through Fargo. He wanted to close his eyes, to relax and let himself enjoy their coupling, but he couldn't, not so long as there was a possible threat nearby. Leaning down, he kissed Delicia's back, running his tongue along her backbone. But when he raised his head, he saw a pair of eyes watching from behind a trunk. Eyes framed by a thatch of raven hair.

Amity knew she had been spotted. Whirling, she bolted, racing off toward the shelf, not once glancing back.

Smiling, Fargo placed his cheek against Delicia's shoulder blade. By now her heaving mounds were hot to the touch. Her nipples were nails, gouging into his palms. He pinched one, then the other. Delicia trembled, breathing heavily as her bottom met his increasingly vigorous thrusts.

"I'm so close, Skye! So close!"

Fargo wasn't. He could go for a good long while yet. And he did, driving into her again and again and again, harder and harder and faster and faster. Suddenly, she uttered a soft cry. They were fused at the waist, two bodies temporarily made one. He didn't slow, never slackening the pace. Pounding even harder, he about lifted her off the ground with each stroke.

"Ohhhhhhhhh!" Delicia started to sag but caught herself. Reaching around behind her, she clutched at his hips and thighs, as if to pull them closer together.

Fargo's mind emptied of all cares. Byers and Harrison and the price on his head were long forgotten. Sensual delight dominated him to the exclusion of all else. All that counted was the rising tide of ecstasy bubbling within. He let himself go, drifting on a sea of carnal pleasure.

"Oh!" Delicia gasped. "Again! I'm exploding again!"

That she did, more violently than the first time, tiny cries escaping her. Fargo couldn't hold back any longer. He lanced up into her as if to cleave her in twain, his manhood throbbing, fit to burst. Again and again he drove into her womanly recesses. His own explosion caused his vision to swim and his heart to hammer like a sledge on quartz. He thought the feeling would never stop, never, ever. But he did, of course, eventually coasting to a gradual stop and standing slumped over, his cheek against her back, his hands still cupping he sagging breasts.

Delicia shook one last time, then said, "I need to sit. Please."

Fargo slid out of her and eased her onto the pine needles. He sank beside her and they lay shoulder to shoulder, the heaving of her breasts matched by the heaving of his own chest. It was a while before their breathing returned to normal.

"You are the most marvelous lover I've ever known," Delicia commented, rolling onto her side so she could rest her head on his shoulder.

"What would your father say?" Fargo asked. The professor was absentminded but he wasn't stupid. Rupert would well guess what they had been up to.

"Not a thing. He knows about my dalliances, as he calls them. But I'm not ready to marry yet. And I can't live without it, if you know what I mean."

Fargo did. Oh, he most certainly did. He idly stroked her long golden hair. "What would your sister say?"

Delicia snorted. "She'd call me a shameless hussy, like she always does. Between you and me, I don't think she's ever been with a man. Not once. If she's not careful, she'll end her days as a lonely, shriveled spinster."

"She's quite pretty," Fargo understated the reality. "Haven't any men shown an interest?"

"Oh, sure. All the time. They warm up to her but she doesn't repay the favor. She treats them as if they're dirt. So naturally they want nothing to do with her." Delicia sighed. "She's a pain in the ass at times, but she's still my sister and I do care for her. I've tried to get her to loosen up, to go out, to do what all the other women do. But she refuses. Perish forbid she should act human for once."

"All this because your mother died?"'

"Our mother was sick for quite a while. She suffered a lot. Amity took it personally. She started saying life was cruel and heartless. That there couldn't be an Almighty because of all the torment we have to bear. And from that day on, she's kept all her feelings bottled up inside of her. She says emotion is for weaklings. I feel pity for her more than anything else. She's missing out on so much life has to offer."

They were quiet for a while, the shadows around them lengthening as the sun began to dip below the mountains.

Fargo roused himself and sat up. He adjusted his clothes, tightened his gunbelt, and brushed off his hat. "We'd better head back."

Delicia put herself together and rose. "I hope we get some time alone again real soon, lover.

You're like ice cream. One scoop just isn't enough."

Her good mood waned some when Fargo retrieved the rabbit. Delicia frowned at the jagged cavity in its head and the blood matting its fur. Holding it by its long legs, Fargo tramped down the slope. Twilight was descending. A solitary star high in the sky was a harbinger of the myriad yet to appear.

"You know," Delicia commented, "I'm beginning to see why you like the wide open spaces so much. The mountains are spectacular."

"Wait until we're higher," Fargo said. She hadn't seen anything yet. Few spectacles rivaled that of being up among the highest peaks, where one was able to see to the ends of the earth, or so it seemed. Being atop a mountain was like being on top of the world. He knew an old mountain man who made it a point to climb to the top of one located near his cabin at least once a month, "to remind me of how much I have in common with gnats," as the oldster phrased it.

When they reached the camp, Professor Cadwell and Amity were by the fire, the professor reading a newspaper, Amity sipping coffee.

"So there you are," Rupert declared. "I was beginning to worry. Afraid we'd have to come looking for you."

Considering that he doubted the man could find a buffalo in a broom closet, Fargo was glad Rupert had stayed put. He wouldn't put it past the professor to become hopelessly lost. Amity, however, was another matter. "How about you?" he baited her. "Were you worried, too?"

"Not one bit," she responded, and smirked. "I've seen how well you can handle yourself."

"And here I thought you didn't notice." Fargo held his own. "You're a bundle of surprises."

"Too bad I can't say the same about you," Amity jousted. "You're just like every other male. You walk around with your brains in your pants."

"Amity!" Professor Cadwell said. "I thought you agreed not to be rude for the duration of our trip."

"Sorry," Amity said, although she didn't sound it. "I couldn't help myself. Some men deserve to be taken down a peg—or three."

Fargo hunkered and drew the Arkansas toothpick. "The same can be said of some women," he remarked. "Especially the ones who think they're better than everyone else."

"Do you mean me?"

"If the shoe fits..." Fargo sliced into the rabbit, gutting it, amused by the grimace that twisted Amity's mouth as the intestines and other organs spilled out. Delicia looked away, unable to bear the gore.

The professor had his face in a *Rocky Mountain News* he had bought on their way out of Denver. "Listen to this. It says that in a few short years, this region will be one of the richest mining districts in the United States. Gold and silver will be extracted from the earth by the ton. Fortunes will be made." Rupert paused. "And to think, we'll be part of history in the making."

"You will?" Fargo said.

Chuckling, the professor folded the paper. "Well, we never know, do we, what the future holds? As a doctor of gemology, I'm inclined to the opinion these mountains hold more than rare minerals. And I hope to prove my theory, with your help."

"But we'll only be up here a few days," Fargo noted. "What can you expect to find in that short a time?"

"One never knows," Rupert said.

Amity lowered her coffee cup. "Remember, Father. There are no guarantees. Perhaps we won't find anything." The way she said it, and the tone she used, gave Fargo the impression she was saying more than was apparent, almost as if she were warning her father not to give too much away.

"I'm well aware of that, daughter," Rupert acknowledged. "But one can always hope, can't one?"

Preparing rabbit stew and biscuits took Fargo half an hour. Soon a mouth-watering aroma filled the clearing. Any lingering squeamishness the women felt over the rabbit evaporated with their rising hunger. Delicia, in particular, couldn't wait for the stew to get done. She balanced the tin plate Fargo had given her on her knees, awaiting her portion, licking her lips every now and again.

Fargo had thickened the broth with flour. He ladled out helpings for the others before filling his own plate and sitting cross-legged to eat. After going all day without food, the stew was delicious beyond words. He dipped a biscuit in the gravy and bit half of it off at once.

"Damn, but you sure can cook, son," Professor Cadwell said, his cheeks bulging like a squirrel stuffed with acorns.

"Who would have thought it?" Amity said insultingly. "Most men can't boil water. How is it you're so talented?"

"Necessity," Fargo said. He could make tasty meals because he *had* to. Often he spent days or weeks on the trail, fending for himself. To spice his food he had learned to add roots and wild onions and herbs and berries. He could take any chunk of meat and serve it any of five different ways; boiled, roasted, fried, dried and salted, and raw.

"Ah, yes," Professor Cadwell said. "Necessity, they say, is the mother of all invention. It's also the inspiration behind many a grand scheme." He gazed ruefully up at the benighted peaks. "It compels us to do things we otherwise never would. To take risks saner men shun. And if the worst comes to pass, all we can do is pray to high heaven that we live to see another day."

Fargo couldn't help but wonder if Rupert was referring to their climb to the talus slopes—or something else entirely.

8

The next day dawned crisp and bright. Skye Fargo served up what was left of the stew along with a fresh batch of coffee. Professor Cadwell was a bundle of nervous energy, so eager to reach the heights that he could barely sit still. Delicia grinned slyly and winked at Fargo as she walked off to wash up. Amity was surly, snapping at everyone for no cause. The professor commented that Fargo should overlook her testiness; she was always disagreeable in the morning. Fargo didn't find it much different from her usual disposition.

It was Delicia's turn to lead the packhorses. Amity rode slouched over, grumbling now and then about how stiff her legs were and how the saddle was chafing them.

Professor Cadwell bubbled with glee. If Fargo thought the man had been gabby the day before, it was nothing compared to the professor's nonstop barrage from the time they started out until Fargo called for a brief rest a noon. Cadwell blubbered about the majesty of the mountains, about the diversity of the wildlife, about the beauty of random wildflowers. When a butterfly fluttered by, the professor squealed like a schoolgirl. "Oh! Mercy! Look there! How lovely! See the yellow and orange? And those wings, how they move!"

Fargo sighed. You would think the man had never seen a butterfly before.

"Do you ever imagine yourself to be one?" Rupert asked him. "Flying gaily along, without a care in the world, a living testament to Nature's splendid artistry? How I envy butterflies. I would give anything to be one, even for a day."

Just at that moment a grayish bird—a shrike, Fargo thought—streaked out of the firs and snatched the butterfly in its beak. It happened so fast that if they had blinked, they would have missed it. In a heartbeat the bird and its meal were gone.

"Just for one day?" Fargo said with a straight face.

Professor Cadwell was outraged. "Did you see that? The gall of some creatures! Devouring my butterfly!"

"It's the way of the wild," Fargo replied. "The survival of the quickest, I like to call it. A good lesson to keep in mind if we come across a predator."

"Oh, that would be sensational!" Rupert exclaimed. "To be able to see a bear or a pack of wolves or a cougar up close has long been a fond dream of mine."

"It might also be the last thing you ever see."

Fargo remembered hearing about a Frenchman, once, a nobleman who came to American with his family and went on a tour of the plains. He brought along as part of his entourage an artist commissioned to sketch and paint whatever the nobleman deemed worthy. One day they came on an old bull buffalo gazing by itself. Since the bull paid no attention to them, the nobleman thought it safe to go up close to it so the artist could do a quick sketch. The nobleman planned to go back to France and show it to all his friends, boasting of the day he stood at arm's length from one of the most massive animals in North America. The bull had other ideas. No sooner did the nobleman turn to the artist and order him to begin than the buffalo charged, its curved horns shearing into the nobleman like hot knives into butter. The nobleman was gored and trampled, his mangled body later brought to St. Louis for proper burial.

"As I noted back in Denver," Professor Cadwell said, "we run risks each and every day of our lives. We can become severely ill. Or waylaid by robbers. Or run over by a carriage. We learn to live with the risks."

"But we shouldn't court them, Father," Amity said. "For once I agree with Mr. Fargo. Tempting fate is stupid. It invites disaster. And I, for one, would like to live to a ripe, old age."

"What for?" retorted Delicia. "You won't have anyone to share your old age with. You'll be all alone, a shriveled prune with no husband, no children, no grandchildren."

They started in again, snipping at one another. Fargo kneed the Ovaro on ahead so he wouldn't have to listen. At midday he called for a halt, largely so the animals could have a rest. He passed a canteen around, then took a drink himself. Pouring some water into his hat, he let the Ovaro wet its muzzle.

Professor Cadwell was watching. "Tell me,

sir. Am I wrong, or are you uncommonly fond of that horse? Last night you rubbed it down and curried it. And now this."

Fargo didn't deny the truth. "This pinto and I have seen a lot of country together. We've been through dust storms, snowstorms, deserts, and swamps. It's saved my life more times than I can recollect. So I guess I do take special care of it. More than most men would."

Amity's interest perked. "You have one redeeming trait, then. I like animals. More than I do any people. Any man who is kind to them can't be all bad."

Delicia made a show of pressing a hand to her heart and another to her forehead. "I must be delirious. Did I hear correctly? My older sister just paid a man a compliment? If we were back in Denver I'd swear you must be drunk."

"Paying a compliment is a far cry from pulling up my skirts for any male who strikes my fancy," Amity countered.

Their squabbling renewed, the two of them verbally clawing at one another like two alley cats. Fargo was reminded more than ever of why he liked to travel alone. Tightening the Ovaro's cinch, he forked leather and told the others to head on out.

From then on the climb was drastically steep, taxing their mounts. Their destination was the mainly barren belt above the tree line where only a few stunted pines and dwarf plants were all that could grow in the rocky soil.

The professor finally shut up. The climb challenged his limited riding ability. There were boulders and logs to be avoided, ruts and steep dropoffs to be shunned.

About two in the afternoon they came to a boulder-strewn slope. Shifting, Fargo warned the others to be on the lookout for rattlesnakes. "They like to sun themselves at this time of day. And they don't always give warning before they strike."

Sure enough, Fargo presently spied a big rattler. He gave it a wide berth, as he did the next, and the one after that. They were halfway to the rim when Amity's bay abruptly nickered and reared. Fargo heard loud rattling as he reined the Ovaro around. A huge snake was coiled on a boulder beside the bay, its head high, its tail shaking violently.

Fargo drew and fired. The rattlesnake's head dissolved in a spray of flesh and gore, but the harm had been done. The bay reared again in terror. Amity gripped the saddle horn to keep from being thrown but she couldn't keep from sliding backward. A sudden bound threw her off balance and she started to fall.

A prick of Fargo's spurs brought the Ovaro alongside. Bending, he grabbed Amity around her waist just as she lost her hold of the saddle horn. Another gig carried them away from the bay, which continued to rear and kick.

Amity was pressed close to his chest, her breasts hard against him, her face so close to his that her breath warmed his cheek. Her eyes widened.

Fargo thought it might be fleeting fear at

her narrow escape, but it was something else, a roiling emotion he couldn't identify. Their gazes locked and she jerked back as if he had slapped her. He nearly lost his grip. Reining the Ovaro to a safe spot, he slowly lowered her to the ground.

Amity had become as stiff as a broom. As Fargo released her, his hand accidentally brushed her ribs and she glanced down sharply, then touched the spot. When she gazed up at him, her face mirrored a peculiar sort of bafflement.

"Are you all right?" Fargo asked.

"Fine," Amity said softly. "It caught me off guard, is all."

"These things usually do." Fargo spurred the pinto to the bay, snagged the bay's reins, and brought it back to her.

Professor Cadwell was mopping his sweaty brow. "That was quick thinking, my friend. We are in your debt."

They resumed their climb. Fargo observed that Amity was exceptionally quiet the rest of the afternoon. He didn't quite know what to make of it. Twice he caught her studying him when she thought he wouldn't catch her. With any other woman the reason would be obvious, but with her there was no telling.

By five o'clock they cleared the heavy timber. High above were the towering cliffs Fargo had glimpsed the day before, only now they were immense, rearing hundreds of feet high and ranging half a mile from north to south. But it was the slopes below the cliffs that most interested Professor Cadwell.

"Look, girls! There they are! Aren't they beautiful!"

Fargo had heard talus described many ways but "beautiful" wasn't one of them. Essentially, it was an accumulation of debris, of loose rock, shale, and dirt that was slick as glass and as insubstantial as quicksand. Horses couldn't keep their footing. Even for a man on foot it was hard to cross without mishap.

Fargo drew rein below the talus. "We'll stay here until it's dark, then head back down into the trees."

"Why can't we camp right where we are?" Rupert asked, already off the mare and flexing his legs to limber them up.

"No wood for a fire for one thing, no water for another." Fargo hooked a leg across his saddle and sat there while the professor scooted to the incline and began to climb. "Be careful," he advised. "That stuff is slippery."

"Have no fear on my account," Rupert said. "I'm more agile than I seem." He proved it by scrambling up onto the talus and then jumping from one large rock to another. "This is perfect, just perfect! The geologic strata are most conducive to our quest."

"Wait for us," Delicia said, hurrying to catch up.

Amity did likewise. She slowed as she went by the stallion and seemed about to say something to Fargo but evidently changed her mind.

"What are you searching for?" Fargo tried one last time.

Professor Cadwell had stooped down and

was lifting rocks to see what was under them. "You'll know soon enough. Until then, I'm afraid it must remain our little secret."

Fargo helped himself to a piece of pemmican and munched while the easterners scurried over the talus, ranging far and wide, lifting more rocks and digging holes. Time and again one or the other slipped but they always got right back up and went on with whatever they were doing. Even Amity, usually so reserved, was swept up in the fever of the hunt and tempted calamity by venturing much higher than her father and sister.

Their antics didn't stop until almost dark. Several times Fargo suggested they head down and pitch camp but the professor always refused, saying, "Just a little longer! Just a little longer!" Only when Delicia bruised a shin after she tripped in the gathering gloom did Rupert call it a day.

All three were caked with dirt from head to toe. Amity swatted at her riding outfit, raising a cloud of dust before she mounted. Professor Cadwell doffed his bowler and slapped it against his legs and jacket.

"Are you ready to head back tomorrow?" Fargo inquired.

"Goodness, no," the professor said. "We haven't found what we're after yet. But the signs are encouraging. The types of rocks we found are consistent with the Diluvial Epoch, which was the primary formative period for the deposits we seek."

"If you say so." It was all Greek to Fargo. To him, rocks were rocks.

A stream flowed near the south end of the talus, its source a channel deep underground. Since they were going to be in the area a day or more, Fargo felt justified in shooting a mule deer. He butchered it and set thick slabs of juicy meat on the fire to roast. The rest he sliced thin and hung over a framework he fashioned from thin branches. None of the Cadwells helped. They were too worn out.

A multitude of stars adorned the heavens by the time the venison was done. Professor Cadwell tore into his steak like a starving wolf, foregoing a fork and knife in favor of his hands. Every few bites he moaned as if in the throes of ecstasy. "Delicious! Simply delicious! Better than any meat I've ever tasted. Your cooking skill is to be commended."

"Definitely," Delicia agreed, her chin glistening with grease. "I thought lobster was the best, but this has it beat." She grinned at Fargo. "You should be a chef."

"Not on your life." Fargo could have told them that he had nothing to do with it, that food cooked outdoors often tasted better than food cooked over a stove or oven, but he was too busy eating.

Amity finally broke her hours-long silence, saying with her mouth full, "Tomorrow could be the day, Father. I found several promising spots."

"So did I," Professor Cadwell said. "It's our extreme fortune that no one else has thought to do as we have done. Once word breaks, we'll be besieged with requests for information. Which reminds me"—he stared at Fargo—"I'd like your solemn word that you'll never divulge where you've brought us."

"What difference does it make?" Fargo asked. Their secretive attitude was beginning to grate on him.

"All the difference in the world," Professor Cadwell said. "The stakes are enormous, more gigantic than you can conceive. So I would take it as a personal favor if you will pledge, right here and now, to keep this location a secret."

Fargo shrugged. "Whatever you want. You're the ones paying me."

"Say it," Rupert insisted. "Give me your word."

"I promise."

Some of Amity's old suspicion flared. "How do we know we can trust him, Father? How do we know he won't run to the *Rocky Mountain News*? Or sell the information to anyone who jingles a few coins in his ear?"

Professor Cadwell bit into his meat, then answered. "I'm surprised at you, my dear. To a man like him, his word is his bond. He could no more break it than he could stomp a helpless puppy to death or beat a woman. Frontiersmen—the best of them, anyhow— live by a certain creed, or code, if you will. They value honor above all else." He looked at Fargo. "Am I right?"

"More or less." Fargo poured himself a cup of coffee. Frontiersmen weren't paragons of virtue by any stretch of the imagination. Some were honorable men, some weren't. They were no better or worse than anyone else.

"It's the less that worries me," Amity said. "We could lose the clothes on our back if we're betrayed. All our planning, the money we've spent, it would be for nothing."

"Have faith, my dear," Rupert said. "Fortune has favored us so far and will continue to do so if we only have faith."

Delicia gazed off down the mountain toward the distant glittering lights of Denver, which from that height seemed as tiny as an anthill. "The first thing I'll do is buy the most expensive dress there is, and a solid gold necklace to go with it. I'll ride to the theater in the finest carriage, and sit in the best seats. Men will fall over themselves to please me. They'll wait on me hand and foot. And when we buy that mansion in New Orleans we've always dreamed of—"

Professor Cadwell coughed. "You're getting a bit carried away with yourself, my dear. First things first, as the saying goes."

"For all we know we might not find a thing," Amity said.

But there was something in how she said it that made Fargo think she was saying it strictly for his benefit. Just as all three of them had been doing all along. They had a secret, a secret that had little to do with the object of their quest. It made Fargo curious, but not curious enough to make an issue of.

Small talk saw them through until almost midnight. The professor revealed he had attended Harvard but later gone on to take courses at Yale. "But my studies are far from complete. I've been considering taking graduate work at Princeton. My credentials as a doctor of gemology are impeccable but there is always room for improvement in one's personal realm of expertise."

Delicia suggested they should go fill the canteen before turning in and gave Fargo a meaningful look. But he didn't take the bait.

"We have enough to last us until morning."

Presently Professor Cadwell crawled under his blankets and was soon snoring loud enough to be heard in Mexico. Delicia, none too pleased, also lay down. Amity, though, lingered over coffee until her sister drifted off. Then she looked up.

"I want to thank you for what you did today."

"My pleasure." Fargo had a sense she had more on her mind than the incident with the rattlesnake.

"You're not like most men I've known. You're not weak or immature, you're not overbearing. You don't treat me as if I'm inferior because I'm female. And you look me squarely in the eyes when you're talking to me."

"I do?" Fargo said, blatantly ogling her chest.

For the first time since they met, Amity laughed. "Touché. I guess I had that coming. I just want you to know it's not you personally. I've been bitter toward men for a good, long while."

"Since the death of your mother?"

"Is that what Delicia told you? No, that's not the reason, although I was deeply upset when she died." Amity took a sip. "You might not believe this, but all my life I've had boys and men interested in me. When I was younger my mother always held them at bay. She protected Delicia and me, kept us out of trouble." Amity took another sip. "But after she died we were suddenly on our own. Besieged by suitors. Delicia was flattered by the attention. She became man crazy. If it weren't for the stigma attached, I honestly believe she would gladly set herself up as a harlot in a luxurious hotel and charge men through the nose for the privilege of bedding her."

"And you?"

Amity didn't answer right away. "I found all the attention men lavished on me tiresome. I resented being pawed, being treated as if I were their personal plaything instead of a person. Twice I had to fight off unwanted advances, once by biting a brute's wrist so hard, I drew blood."

Fargo added a limb to the fire. He would keep it blazing most of the night to discourage roving predators.

"So I grew to dislike men," Amity disclosed. "To strongly resent them. I wasn't about to be like my sister. The few times I was attracted to one, I banished the thought from my mind and took a lot of cold baths."

"Sorry to hear that," Fargo said, stretching out on his blanket with his head resting on his saddle.

"You are? Why?"

"Like your sister said, you'll end your days a spinster, and no one—" The unexpected crackling of undergrowth brought Fargo to his feet with the Henry in hand. Something was coming through the trees toward their camp, something big.

"What is it?" Amity whispered, sliding over beside him.

Fargo didn't know, not until the rasp of heaving breathing and a ponderous tread identified it to his trained ears. "A bear."

"Lord, no! What kind?"

Two reddish eyes appeared, gleaming embers reflecting the firelight. Their height and spacing suggested they belonged to the last beast Fargo wanted to encounter. "It's a grizzly."

Amity snatched her purse, frantically dug for her derringer, and pointed it at the massive beast.

"Don't," Fargo said, placing a hand on her wrist. "You'd only make it mad. Stand still and maybe it will go away."

No such luck. The brute lumbered closer, its shaggy coat dappled by shadows and dancing light. Lifting its great head, the grizzly tested the air, sniffing noisily.

"If it attacks, get your father and sister out of here," Fargo whispered.

"What about you?"

The bear ambled to the edge of the clearing. Its gigantic head swung from side to side, its nostrils flaring. A paw the size of a ham, tipped by thick claws, raked the earth like the hoof of a bull about to charge. Fargo glanced at the horse string, afraid one would act up and spur the grizzly into rushing them.

"It's so huge," Amity said in awe.

Grizzlies invariably were. Full grown, they stood five feet high at the shoulders and tipped the scales to over a thousand pounds. With their bulk and pronounced humps, they were monstrous up close, so frightening that those who saw them for the first time often froze up, making easy prey of themselves.

Fargo sighted on the bear's chest. Their thick skulls were proof against most slugs, even those of large-caliber guns. He didn't want to shoot if he could help it. A wounded grizzly was a living engine of fury, virtually unstoppable. He'd once seen a silvertip plow into a group of mountain men who put fifteen bullets into it before it finally collapsed.

"It's coming closer!" Amity gasped.

The bear's enormous head and powerful shoulders were fully visible now. And its reddish eyes were fixed right on them.

Fargo had his finger on the Henry's trigger. He might be able to get off three shots before the bear reached him, but that wouldn't be enough. Not with one that size. He could now smell the musty scent of its coat.

For terrible seconds the outcome hung in the balance. Then Professor Cadwell rolled over onto his side and snorted in his sleep.

Instantly, the grizzly spun and vanished, melting into the gloom. It was hard to believe anything so immense could move so quietly, yet it never made any sound. It was there one second, gone the next.

Fargo slowly lowered the Henry. Bears were wildly unpredictable, as this one had just demonstrated. The slightest strange noise might spook them, or incite an attack. He let out a breath he hadn't realized he had been holding and set the Henry's stock on the ground. "That was a close one."

The next moment Amity was in his arms. She pressed her face to his chest, trembling uncontrollably, like a child who had experienced a horrible nightmare. Fargo was stunned. He stroked her raven hair until her fright passed. When she stepped back, she had regained control.

"I'm sorry. I don't know what came over me."

"The first time I saw one, I nearly fainted," Fargo fibbed.

Amity regarded him intently. "Somehow I doubt that very much. You weren't scared just now. I could tell."

"I've run into grizzlies before."

"It's more than that," Amity said. "I could meet up with one of those monsters every day for the rest of my life and each time I would be as petrified as I was just now." She shook her head. "No, it's you. You're a very courageous man."

Fargo grinned. "Better be careful. That makes two compliments in one day. I don't know if I can stand the shock."

Again Amity laughed.

"You should do that more often," Fargo said. "You're beautiful when you're not mad at the world and everyone in it."

Amity averted her face. "I think I'll turn in. This night has been full of surprises, and I don't need another. Not now. Not when we're so close to achieving our dream. I'm sorry, Skye. I've misjudged you. If nothing else, I've learned I'm human like everyone else. Much too late, I'm afraid. Tomorrow, everything changes."

Fargo watched her lie down and cover herself, turning so her back was to him. She had given him a lot to ponder. He stayed up several more hours in case the grizzly took it into its head to return, but it never did. Even so, when he turned in he kept the rifle at his side. A man could never be too careful. The last sound he heard before he drifted off was the lonesome wail of a wolf from up toward the talus, a cry borne on the breeze down across the rolling slopes and off toward the domain of men far below.

9

The search resumed at seven o'clock the next morning. The professor couldn't wait to reach the talus slopes and kept urging his daughters to hurry up. After a quick breakfast of pemmican and coffee, Fargo saddled the horses and off they went. He took the packhorses along as a precaution. Mountain lions loved horseflesh, and there was always the possibility of a stray band of Indians or outlaws happening by and not being able to resist temptation.

Professor Cadwell handed out leather pouches to Amity and Delicia, slung the strap of a third over his shoulder, and marched on up the talus, beaming like a child on a birthday. The three of them roamed back and forth, up and down, digging, lifting rocks, occasionally slipping and sometimes falling but never giving up in their mysterious quest.

Fargo sat on a flat boulder at the bottom and watched their antics in bemusement. They brought to mind the frenzy of gold seekers fresh on the scent of a rich vein. He noticed how every so often one or the other would partly raise a large rock and grope around underneath it. An hour and a half had elapsed, or thereabouts, when the professor raised his hands to the azure sky and shouted like a madman.

"Eureka! I've found some! I've found some!" Rupert hopped up and down in the throes of elation, only to stumble and pitch to his knees when the shifting talus gave way.

Fargo was instantly on his feet. The rivulets of earth and stone might turn into a torrent, sweeping the professor to the bottom and dashing him against scattered boulders. But the mercurial talus stopped dribbling and Cadwell regained his footing.

Father and daughters converged, all grinning like cats that had just caught plump mice. When Professor Cadwell reached solid ground, he rushed toward Fargo, his palm held out. "See! See them for yourself!"

In the professor's hand were several walnut-sized objects, slightly whitish and almost transparent, each with many lustrous sides. Rupert fondled them as he might a lover, showing more teeth than a bear eating honey.

"What are they?" Fargo asked.

"You don't know?" Rupert rejoined, as if it should be obvious. "These are *diamonds,* my boy! Genuine diamonds! When cut and polished, I should hazard a guess these three will be worth in excess of fifty thousand dollars."

Amity and Delicia came running over. Each handled the precious stones, Delicia licking one with the tip of her tongue as if tasting it.

"Do you realize the significance of this momentous find?" Professor Cadwell said, facing the talus and extending his arms. "We're rich! Rich, I tell you, girls! Wealthy beyond our wildest dreams!"

Fargo surveyed the slopes. "Do you think there are more?"

"I know there are!" the professor boomed. "Where there's one diamond, invariably there are hundreds, sometimes thousands! And unlike some of the diamond finds elsewhere on the globe, these don't need to be mined. Not at first, anyway. All we need to do is sift through the talus to find them."

"Our dream has come true," Delicia said softly.

Amity, however, was strangely quiet. She rolled one of the diamonds between her fingers, her brow furrowed.

Rupert turned. "We can't let word of this leak out. Not a peep to anyone until I've filed a proper claim." He looked at Fargo. "I want you to promise me again that you won't betray our trust."

The request angered Fargo, and his anger must have been obvious because Cadwell hastily went on.

"Not that I would ever think you capable of so heinous a deed. I merely ask out of concern that my darling girls will be deprived of their rightful reward if news of our discovery leaks prematurely. Please don't be offended."

"I already gave you my word," Fargo reminded him.

"That you did. Blame my zeal on my excitement." Grinning, the professor hugged both women. "Then it's back to Denver we go! Soon the three of us will be rightfully famous! And soon, very soon, I can give you girls all the wonderful things I've always dreamed of giving you."

The professor insisted on leaving right that minute. Fargo suggested they have a small meal to tide them over until nightfall but Rupert wouldn't hear of it. Any delay, however trifling, was unacceptable.

"Greatness and vast wealth waits for no man!" he declared. "The sooner we reach Denver, the sooner I can file a claim. Onward! Downward! Let us make all due haste!"

So they did. It was the professor's turn to lead the packhorses but Fargo decided to do it himself. It was broad daylight and there had been no sign of hostiles. He brought up the rear, alert as always. Several times Amity glanced back at him as if she wanted to say something, but she never did.

Dense forest closed in around them, making the going slow. Fargo had to repeatedly steer

Cadwell in the right direction because the professor kept straying to the north or south. About the fifth or sixth time, Rupert glanced back and said, "I never could get it straight in my head whether the sun rose in the east and set in the west or the other way around."

This from a man with university degrees.

Noon found them traversing a switchback. They could see for miles, clear down to the Emerald Foothills and the vast plain beyond. Denver was a brown smudge against a backdrop of green.

At the bottom of the switchback the ground leveled off for fifty or sixty yards. Fargo hollered for Rupert to rein up. One of the packs was loose. Climbing down, Fargo tightened the rope that held the load in place. As he stepped to the Ovaro to fork leather, he saw that the professor's hands were in the air, and that Amity and Delicia were unnaturally rigid.

"Don't move a muscle, mister!"

Three men with rifles had Fargo covered. They fanned out, the tall gunman in the center, aiming at Fargo's head.

"Unbuckle your gunbelt and let it drop. Try anything fancy and you'll regret it."

Fargo almost went for his pistol anyway. He figured he could draw and snap off a couple of shots before the trio had time to react, but the Cadwells were in front of him. They might be hit if the gunman sprayed lead. So he did as he was instructed.

"That's damn obliging of you, mister," the tall gunman said. He wore a slicker common in cow country and had a Texas twang.

The gunman on the right, a weasel-like character whose clothes were filthy and whose face even worse, snapped, "What the hell are we waitin' for Bodeen? Let's make wolf meat of them."

Bodeen glanced at the weasel. "We'll do it my way, Trent. I'm the one who rustled up this job, ain't I? Unless you reckon you'd like to be top dog from here on out."

Trent licked his slit of a mouth. "Hell, I ain't addlepated. What you say goes. It always has."

"Same with me," the third man chimed in.

"Cover Fargo," Bodeen directed. Lowering his rifle, he stepped to the mare. "Climb on down, potgut. I don't rightly cotton to what we have to do, but five hundred dollars is five hundred dollars."

"What is this about?" Professor Cadwell asked. "Are you robbers?"

"Hell, no." Bodeen was offended. "We're hired guns, mister. Assassins, the papers calls us."

Rupert slid from the saddle. "You kill people for money?"

"Now you're catching on." Bodeen motioned at the women. "You, too, ladies. I'm right sorry about this. I reckon you're just in the wrong place at the wrong time. If I'd know women were involved..." He shrugged.

Amity clasped her traveling bag to her as if she were afraid. "Don't tell me you intend to harm us? What have we ever done to you?"

"Why are you doing this?" Delicia threw in.

Bodeen didn't look none too happy. "Didn't you hear me? For five hundred dollars. That's the bounty on this jasper's head." He nodded at Fargo.

Professor Cadwell took a step toward the Texan, only to freeze when Bodeen pointed the rifle at his midsection. "But what does that have to do with us? There is no bounty on our heads."

"There can't be witnesses," Bodeen said.

Amity's right hand was inches above the opening to her bag. "You would murder a pair of innocent women?"

Bodeen frowned. "Lady, for five hundred dollars I'd put windows in the skull of my own sister."

Trent was fidgeting like a rat eager to bite into cheese. "Damn it all! Enough stalling. Let's shoot them and be done with it."

In their preoccupation with the Cadwells, the gunmen had forgotten about Fargo. His hands had been resting on the saddle but now he slowly lowered them to his side and began to bend at the knees. Cadwells or not, he had to do something before the gunmen opened fire.

Delicia bestowed her most intoxicating smile on the tall Texan. "You'd really kill me? What kind of man are you?" She moved a bit to the left, partially blocking Bodeen's view of her sister.

"It's nothing personal, ma'am."

Professor Cadwell was indignant. "How despicable! You don't strike me as the kind of person who goes around brutally slaying others. Where is your conscience, sir? Where is your innate human decency? My daughters are my prides and joys. Don't harm them. I beseech you, one man to another."

"Don't," Bodeen said harshly.

Fargo saw Amity's right hand slide into her traveling bag. He glanced down at his holster, and at the Colt, which had slid partway out when he dropped the gunbelt.

Trent stamped a foot. "I'm tried of all this jawin', Bodeen. If you don't have the gumption to buck these females out in gore, say the word and I'll gladly do the honors. Men, women, old, young, it don't make no nevermind to me. It's just like swattin' flies, far as I'm concerned."

The Texan hesitated. He gazed at Delicia, at her shimmering golden hair and her ripe red lips and voluptuous figure, and he balked, his rifle angled downward. "You're the prettiest filly I ever did see," he remarked. "I'm going to regret killing you."

"How sweet of you," Delicia said, her smile widening. "It's a pity, though, I can't say the same." And with that she dropped into a crouch, squalling at the top of her lungs, "Now, sis! Now!"

Amity whipped out her derringer and trained it on Bodeen. The Texan's jaw slackened, and for a span of seconds he was too stunned to move. Then he galvanized to life, but as he brought his Spencer up, the derringer cracked.

Trent and the other assassin made the mistake of swiveling toward their friend.

141

Crouching, Fargo grabbed the Colt. It boomed twice and at each blast a gunman was impaled by sizzling lead. The other assassin dropped but Trent merely staggered. Fargo shot him again as Trent tried to raise his rifle, then a third time as Trent staggered and tripped, and then sank to the grass with reddish foam flecking his mouth.

Bodeen was also down but not quite dead. His fingers clutched convulsively at the Spencer but he couldn't quite reach it. As Fargo's shadow fell across him his brown eyes drifted upward. "A woman! Can you believe it? Did you see what she did?"

"I saw," Fargo said.

"Never reckoned on being done in like this," the Texan said glumly. "I'm downright ashamed of myself."

"Who hired you? Who's offering the five hundred?"

Bodeen didn't seem to hear. "I always thought it would be a faster gunhand. Maybe an Injun. Or an animal."

Fargo bent down. "I need to know who put the bounty on my head."

"Who else?" Bodeen said, and coughed. "Talk about a damned stupid way to die." Moments later he did, expiring with an expression of puzzlement on his rugged, tanned face.

Fargo slapped his leg in frustration. This made three times hired guns had tried to rub him out, three times luck had smiled on him. No man's luck held forever, though. He *had* to find out who was behind it before his did.

Amity was reloading her derringer. "They weren't very professional, were they? All that talking, when they should have shot us down from ambush. For all their bluster, they were amateurs. But it worked in our favor, didn't it?"

How was it, Fargo wondered, that she was suddenly so knowledgeable about paid killers and the like? And why wasn't she the least bit upset at having just killed another human being? If he didn't know better—and he didn't—he might think she had done it before. More than once. "You took a big gamble."

"What was the alternative? Let them shoot us?" Amity shoved the derringer into her bag. "Be serious."

Fargo went through their pockets. He came across no notes or anything else that would tell him who was responsible. Like the gunmen in the hotel, each had a roll of bills totaling fifty dollars. Money paid in advance was his guess.

"How do you suppose they found us?" Professor Cadwell asked.

"They probably tracked us from Denver and were biding their time ever since," Fargo speculated.

"Well, all's well that ends with us alive and in one piece, eh?" Rupert dismissed them with a wave of a pudgy hand. "We needn't concern ourselves with a decent burial. Scavengers will dispose of the remains. And time is of the essence."

Fargo couldn't get over how perfectly calm the three Cadwells were. As if they took part in shootouts every day of the week and twice on Saturdays. "We'll dig shallow graves for them," he said.

"Why bother?" Delicia asked. "They wouldn't have given us the same courtesy, and you know it."

"She's right," Rupert said. "Why tire ourselves over these vermin? If we push real hard we can almost reach the foothills by dark."

Fargo slowly rose. His fondness for them was fast fading. "We can spare ten minutes. With all four of us digging, it shouldn't take much more than that." He scoured the grass for a suitable spot.

Professor Cadwell made a sound like a goose having its neck wrung. "I really must protest most vigorously! We bear tidings the entire world waits breathlessly to hear. The greatest gemological discovery in the history of this great country! Why delay over a mere trifle?"

Amity surprised Fargo by saying, "Skye is right, Father. I killed one of these men. All of us should pitch in to bury them."

"*Et tu?*" Rupert said, exasperated. "Very well. If you insist on this silliness, we'll plant them and be done with it so we can be on our way."

It took twenty minutes, not ten. The professor had little enthusiasm for the work, Delicia even less. Afterward, Fargo turned to them and said, "Now we need to find their mounts."

Rupert looked fit to lay an egg. "Another

delay? I can't believe this. All my years of seeking and striving! And now, with success in my grasp, I must twiddle my thumbs while we indulge in frivolous pursuits."

"If the horses are tied somewhere, they could starve to death," Fargo mentioned.

"So? What's another horse, more or less?" Professor Cadwell said. "The West is full of them. But diamonds, now that's another story!"

Fargo led the pack animals into the nearest trees. He didn't have to search far. Three tired mounts were indeed tied to low limbs. Unraveling more rope, he added them to their own string, at the rear. Then he fell in behind the others as a joyous Professor Cadwell started briskly down the mountain.

Amity hung back until the stallion was abreast of her bay. "I saw the look on your face. Please don't hold it against my father. He's worked so hard to make his dream come true."

"Most people do."

"But they don't have to put up with the ridicule and abuse he has. For years he's maintained there had to be a diamond deposit somewhere in these mountains. His peers laughed him to scorn. Now he can prove to them he was right."

Fargo looked at her. Her bosom was tight against her blouse, her breasts bobbing with every step the bay took. "What do you get out of this? Besides being rich."

"Isn't that enough?" Amity brushed strands of hair from her face. "I still can't quite believe it. After being poor my whole life, to suddenly have more money than I'll ever need will take some getting used to. I just hope—" She caught herself.

"Hope what?" Fargo prompted.

"I just hope nothing goes wrong. I don't want my father's crowning glory to be snatched away from him."

Fargo had the impression she intended to say something else. "I won't be around to see it. As soon as you hand over the rest of my money, I'm leaving Denver."

"So soon?" Amity sounded disappointed. "I was hoping you'd stick around a while. To make up for how I've behaved, I was going to treat you to a meal. Or a drink."

"How about both?" A meal wouldn't take that long, and then Fargo could point the Ovaro north. But he didn't like the idea of running away from a fight. As he thought about it he realized he'd much rather find out who was to blame for the bounty on his head and show them what he thought of their brainstorm. But every hour he lingered gave money-hungry gun sharks sixty more minutes in which to earn the bounty. Sixty more chances to fill him with lead. And sixty more chances for innocent bystanders to take slugs meant for him.

"We have a deal," Amity declared. The sun, bathing her face at just the right angle, accented her natural beauty, lending her cheeks a warm, rosy sheen. Gone was the icy exterior, the frigid stare. She had undergone an amazing transformation. But was

146

the change permanent, or only temporary?

On the way back to town, the professor's mouth appeared to have come unhinged. He talked and talked and talked, and then talked some more. He went on and on about the prestige he would earn, about the riches soon to be his. Toward sunset he glanced at Fargo and commented, "I won't forget your part in this, either, my friend. We owe this all to you."

"You're the one who knew where to find the diamonds," Fargo responded.

Rupert then said something that struck Fargo as strange. "Perhaps. But none of this would have been possible without you. You are the linchpin on which our entire gambit depended. You have my undying gratitude."

The professor was so worked up, he hardly ate a bite. He sat by the crackling flames, rubbing and stroking the diamonds in his palm, his face lit by a gleam that had no relation to the fire.

Much later, after everyone except Fargo was sound asleep, he opened the professor's saddlebags and took out the three leather pouches the Cadwells had carried around up on the talus. All three were empty. Or so Fargo thought until he started to pull his hand from the last one and his little finger brushed what felt like a pebble. He took it out and held it in the light.

The small diamond's lustrous surfaces sparkled brightly. Fargo held it awhile, turning it over and over in his hand even as he turned over and over in his mind what finding it meant. He glanced at the professor and at the two women, and then replaced the diamond in the pouch and put all three bags back where they had been.

A sliver of moon rose in the east and was midway across the celestial vault before Fargo turned in. He was troubled, deeply so. He realized he couldn't leave Denver as soon as he'd like. Not now.

. The next morning Professor Cadwell was up before anyone, even Fargo. They drank coffee, chewed more pemmican, and then were off, pressing on until they reached the foothills, where they stopped long enough for the animals to quench their thirst.

The sight of Denver, so close it seemed they could reach out and touch it, fueled the professor's gift for gab. Fargo spent most of the morning listening to Rupert go on and on about different kinds of diamonds and how to tell valuable stones from worthless ones. Fargo paid little interest until a certain fact was mentioned.

"The monumental importance of our discovery can't be stressed enough. Diamonds have only been found in three other places. In India, where some of exceptional size have been unearthed. In the interior of Brazil. And, I have heard, in California, during the gold rush. A few were even found at placer mines, but only a few."

"Will you sell your diamonds as they are?" Fargo inquired.

"Oh, dear me, no," Professor Cadwell said. "Diamonds must be cut and polished. Any competent jeweler could do it, but most of

148

those found in other countries are funneled through Holland, where some of the best diamond cutters in the world live."

Late in the afternoon they arrived at the city's outskirts. The professor said he had a lot to attend to and asked Fargo if he would mind tending to the horses. "No, you go on ahead," Fargo answered, happy to give his ears a rest. The Cadwells hailed a carriage and clattered off, Delicia leaning out the window to grin and wave at him.

Now Fargo had eight horses to lead. What with the volume of traffic, it took him an hour to get to the stable. The owner refused to put up the three mounts belonging to the gunmen unless Fargo paid for a day's stabling in advance, which Fargo refused to do. He put the Ovaro in its stall and fed it oats, then asked direciton to the marshal's office.

Tom Hendly was there, leaning against a post out front, prying at his teeth with a toothpick when Fargo tied the three gunmen's horses to the hitch rail.

"Presents for you."

The lawman stuck the toothpick in the corner of his mouth. "For me?" He listened to how Fargo happened to come by them, then commented, "They had to be more of Charley Harrison's bunch. That makes seven you've accounted for since you hit town. At the rate you're going, in another month he won't have any men left."

Fargo had something more important to discuss. "Have you learned who put the bounty on me yet?"

"No. Sorry. I've asked around. But my usual sources haven't heard a thing. It has to be Harrison, though. Who else could it be?"

That was the question Fargo mulled over on his way to the hotel. A barbershop caught his eye and he stopped in for a bath and a trim. While he soaked in an oversized washtub, the barber's heavyset wife carried his buckskins out back, hung them over a line, and wacked them with her broom, raising billowy puffs of dust.

It was nearly sunset when Fargo emerged, scrubbed clean and smelling of the lavender-scented oil the barber had combed through his hair. He checked behind him often but no one was following. Whoever wanted him dead probably didn't know he was back yet, which worked to Fargo's advantage. He would lay low, only coming out at night to hunt down the person hunting him.

Fargo came to a corner and paused to let a wagon laden with household items go by. A street urchin was hawking the *Rocky Mountain News*.

"Read all about it!" the kid bawled. "Hot off the presses! The latest edition!" He tugged at Fargo's sleeve. "How about you, mister? Want to read about the new strike?"

"Where did they find gold this time?" Fargo asked as he fished some coins from his pocket, the urchin didn't say. Snatching the money, the boy dashed toward another potential customer.

"Read all about it! Greatest find yet!"

Grinning, Fargo unfolded the newspaper.

His grin faded. In big, bold letters was the headline: FAMOUS SCOUT DISCOVERS DIAMONDS! Under it, in smaller print, he read, TRAILSMAN MAKES FIND OF THE CENTURY! Fargo was stupefied. It couldn't be! He told himself.

Yet there it was, in bold black and white.

10

Skye Fargo barreled into the offices of the *Rocky Mountain News* with the copy he had bought ten minutes ago crumpled in his hand, lightning flashing in his eyes. He spotted William Byers at a desk at the back and stalked past a startled typesetter who came over to ask if he could be of any help. Byers was scribbling in a ledger and didn't look up until Fargo was almost to the desk. Then it was the editor's turn to be startled, but, composing himself, Byers rose to offer his hand.

"Why, Mr. Fargo, what a pleasant surprise."

Fargo didn't shake. He threw the paper on the desk and snapped, "What the hell did you think you were doing?"

Byers was perplexed. "I beg your pardon?" he said, unfolding the copy. "Ah. You mean our lead story? By now it's spreading like wildfire throughout the city. Your fame will increase by leaps and bounds."

Placing both hands on the desk, Fargo bent toward him. "You made it sound as if I discovered those diamonds, and I didn't. I want you to write a retraction."

William Byers scratched his head. "Is that what has you so flustered? We'll talk this over. I really can't understand why you're so upset." He indicated a chair. "Have a seat, why don't you?"

"I'll stand," Fargo growled. It was all he could do to keep from leaping over the desk and slugging the man. He never had been fond of journalists, or, to be more precise, of their habit of distorting the truth. Evidently the *News*'s owner was just like all the others, a huckster who fabricated tales to sell more papers.

Byers was growing worried. "Please, calm yourself. You did lead the Cadwell expedition, did you not? And you did find diamonds up in the mountains, true?" He tapped the newspaper Fargo had bought. "That's news! A major story. All I did was print it. What's wrong with that?"

Fargo had read the article all the way through. It contained so many factual errors that he didn't know where to begin. "There wasn't an *expedition*. It was just Professor Cadwell, his daughters, and me. They were the ones who found the stones, not me. You made it sound as if I knew right where to lead them, as if the whole idea was mine."

"I only related the details as they were related to me." Byers sat down and opened a small drawer on the right. From it he took a brown notebook which he placed in front of him. "I have my notes right here. I always keep a record of interviews I conduct. Less chance of a mistake creeping into my copy that way!"

Fargo's anger was draining away. He snatched the chair, swung it around, and sat with his arms folded across the back. "Let me hear what Cadwell told you."

"Ah. Here it is. He came in all excited and told me to brace myself for the story of the century." Byers stopped flipping pages. "Then he showed me the diamonds, and claimed they were found right up in the Rockies. I was skeptical. Who wouldn't be? But he told me that you served as guide on their expedition, and showed me his credentials. A degree from Harvard, and another from Albany, attesting to the fact he's a doctor of gemology." Byers paused. "How could I not print it? We were almost ready to go to press with the regular edition, but I had my people stop the presses and added an account of the discovery. Cadwell was right. It *is* the story of the century."

"And he claimed I knew exactly where to find the diamonds?"

"Not in so many words. He implied as much, though. He made it sound as if they would never have found them without you. So that was the slant I used." Byers waved away a subordinate who was approaching. "How can you blame me? You're famous. People have read all about you. They know you're a man of your word. So if you say there are diamonds in the Rockies, they know it to be true."

Fargo had a thought. "Did you have the diamonds checked?"

"Do you take me for an idiot? Of course! I sent a runner to a jeweler down the street and asked him to verify they were real. He examined them right here, in front of Cadwell and myself, and assured me they were genuine diamonds of medium to high purity. They'll make excellent gems when polished and cut."

Now that his anger had evaporated, Fargo felt a twinge of regret. He couldn't blame Byers for reporting the story as Cadwell had related it. If anyone were to blame, it was Rupert himself. But the professor might not have done it on purpose. Given Rupert's flair for the dramatic and his tendency to exaggerate, it was no wonder the newspaper's account contained mistakes.

"Professor Cadwell has graciously consented to take myself and a few other prominent citizens up to the diamond fields in a couple of days," Byers revealed. "He said you might be willing to guide us, but he was sure he could find them again by himself if need be. He's already filed a claim."

So they were diamond *fields* now? Fargo thought.

"The professor also asked if I could print up certificates of stock he plans to issue in the mining company he's forming. The money he raises from the sales of the certificates will be used to buy machinery and hire the men needed to get the operation going."

"Do you think he'll have any takers?"

"Oh, Lord, yes. He'll have to fight them off with a pitchfork. He's promising triple the return on every investment. Twenty-five thousand dollars a share might sound steep, but not for all those in Denver who have acquired small fortunes from gold and silver. I daresay he'll sell all the certificates he has within a day or two of announcing the venture."

"Did he say how much he wants to raise?"

"He'd like to have half a million in ready cash at the outset, but I expect he'll double that figure. Or more. The sky's the limit. By this time next week, your friend Cadwell could well be a millionaire. And that's before he even digs another diamond out of the ground."

"That much?" Fargo said. So the professor had been right. The Cadwells were going to be rich beyond their wildest dreams.

"Yes. And he owes it all to you. Or, I should say, to your reputation. The people who invest in his company won't do it based on Cadwell's word alone. They'll do it in large measure because of your connection with the venture. Because of the man you are, and the trust you inspire."

An awful thought occurred to Fargo. He submerged it but it immediately resurfaced. Shaking his head, he refused to consider the possibility, yet he couldn't rid himself of the memory of the small diamond he had found in Amity's pouch.

William Byers's voice dropped. "It's a good thing the Committee of Safety didn't string you up the other night. Once word of the diamonds spreads back East, Denver will grow by leaps and bounds. Gold brought argonauts by the thousands. Diamonds will bring them by the tens of thousands. Our city will prosper like never before. All thanks to you."

"I'm glad."

"You don't sound glad."

Fargo rose. "If you should see Cadwell before I do, tell him I'll lead however many he wants up to the diamond fields the day after tomorrow."

"You will? Yet a few minutes ago you made it sound as if you wanted nothing more to do with his venture. Quite frankly, you have me confused." Byers came around the desk. "I'll see you to the door, if you don't mind. There's something else we must discuss."

"There is?"

"Marshal Hendly has told me about the price on your head. Only Charley Harrison would be so bold. We can't let him succeed, especially not now. You're a vital part of Denver's future, and I, for one, don't want anything to happen to you. With your permission, I'd like to assign some of the Committeemen to guard you."

Fargo let the idea sink in. The same vigilantes who had tried to kill him just days ago would now be protecting him? Life could be too ridiculous for words at times. "No."

"I urge you to reconsider. If not for your sake alone, then for the sake of this city I love so dearly."

"I can watch my own back. I don't need nursemaiding."

They shook and Fargo departed. He took

side streets and alleys back to his hotel in case more money-hungry gunmen made another try on his life.

The stuffy desk clerk was pacing behind the counter. When Fargo entered, he hissed and beckoned.

"Come here! Come here!" he whispered. "Quick! Hurry!"

The lobby was empty, but Fargo rested his hand on the Colt as he crossed. The clerk kept glancing at the stairs as if afraid a swarm of painted warriors were about to pour down them. "What's wrong?"

"I'm not supposed to tell you this. He warned me that if I did, he'd have every bone in my body broken." The clerk wrung his hands. "There's a man waiting for you up in your room. He made me give him the spare key. I'm sorry."

"This man have a name?"

"He didn't give one."

"What does he look like?" Fargo suspected it was Ike Talbot, which suited him just fine. It was time to end it, one way or another.

"He's big, real big, about as big as you are. He wears black and has a beard. I think he's from the South somewhere because he had a drawl like those Southerners do."

The description fit only one person Fargo knew. "Charley Harrison," he said aloud.

"Oh, Lord. Is that who it is?" The clerk clenched his fingers so tight, his knuckles were white. "And I've gone and disobeyed him! He'll have me beaten, I just know it. Or maybe gutted and left to die!"

"Calm down," Fargo said. "I won't tell him you told me."

Tears of joy trickled from the clerk's eyes. "Thank you! Oh, thank you!" He gripped Fargo's hand and pumped it. "Do you want me to run and fetch the marshal?"

"Is Harrison alone?"

"So far as I know. No one was with him when he came in and I haven't seen anyone other than guests go up since he got here." The clerk glanced toward a hallway on the left. "Even if someone snuck in the back way they'd have to go by me."

"Thanks." Fargo gave him ten dollars. He'd earned it.

As silently as possible, Fargo climbed to the landing. A few boards creaked underfoot but not loudly enough to give him away. He listened at his door but heard no unusual sounds. Stepping to one side, he inserted the key, then quickly turned it and pushed.

"Come on in. I've been waiting for you."

Charley Harrison had moved the chair to the middle of the room. He sat with his hands on his knees. He wasn't holding a gun, nor was there a holster around his waist. On the dresser was the spare room key which Fargo pretended not to notice.

Warily entering, Fargo closed the door and leaned against it. "How did you get in here?"

"The young gent at the front desk can be mighty accommodating with a little persuasion. I've heard you were back, and it was important that I talk to you in private."

"I'm listening."

Harrison didn't bandy words. "The five hundred dollars being offered for your hide is common knowledge. I know attempts have already been made, and more might be. So I wanted to tell you to your face that I have nothing to do with it."

"And you expect me to believe you on your word alone?" For all Fargo knew, Harrison's visit was a ruse to throw him off the scent.

"No. I want you to consider a few things. For starters, what could I possibly hope to gain by having you murdered? We had an agreement, an understanding, and I stand to lose a lot more than you do if I break it." Harrison frowned. "I have enough problems to deal with without adding one more. Byers and his damnable vigilantes are putting more pressure on me every day. If I were to put a bounty on anyone's head, it would be his. Not yours."

Again Fargo was struck by the man's seeming sincerity. But polished liars were masters of deceit. How could he be sure Harrison was telling the truth? "Did you have two men on your payroll by the names of Bodeen and Trent?"

"No, but I've seen them in the Criterion a few times. They recently came up the trail from Texas and were looking for work. Why? Did they say they work for me?"

"No," Fargo admitted.

Charley Harrison stood. "Well, I've said all I had to. I'm been trying to find out who put the bounty on you but no one seems to know anything. All I know for sure is that the offer is legitimate."

Fargo moved aside so Harrison could leave.

"One more thing. This diamond business. It's another reason I would never have you shot."

"How do you figure?"

"The diamonds are going to lure pilgrims to Denver in record numbers. There will be more sheep to fleece, more pots for me to dip my fingers into." Harrison smirked. "I want you alive, mister. You're one of the few people who know where the diamonds are, and those stones are the best thing that could happen to me."

After the door closed Fargo sat on the bed, his chin on his hands. Everything Harrison said made sense. Ironically, it mirrored William Byers's own sentiments. Both men saw the diamonds as the greatest boon to the city since gold was discovered. Neither wanted anything to happen to him.

All of which left Fargo no closer to learning who desired him dead. Rather than endlessly rehash it in his head, he stretched out to catch some sleep. Unfortunately, sleep eluded him. After a while he gave up and rose. A visit to a saloon was in order. He'd treat himself to a few drinks, the willing company of a friendly dove, maybe a hand or two of cards. He opened the door—and thought he must be seeing things.

"Surprised?" Amity Cadwell asked.

Surprise didn't begin to describe how Fargo felt. "How long have you been standing out here?"

"Four or five minutes. I couldn't get up the courage to knock." Amity wore a beige dress adorned with ribbons and frills that contrasted beautifully with her long raven tresses. A silver necklace and matching silver earrings lent extra appeal.

"Afraid I'd bite?" Fargo teased.

"No. Afraid you would kiss me."

Before Fargo could respond, Amity flung herself at him and mashed her cherry mouth against his, kissing him so hard it produced more pain than pleasure. It was as if she were trying to make up for all the romance she had missed out on over the years. Fargo gently pushed on her shoulders. "Whoa, there! Not so fast. Are you sure about this?"

Amity was breathing heavily, her cheeks scarlet, her bosom heaving. "I've never been so sure of anything in my life."

Fargo wasn't convinced. "But—" he began.

"Hush." Amity placed a finger against his lips. "Didn't anyone ever tell you not to look a gift horse in the mouth?" She pressed him back and kicked the door shut. "I only have an hour, Skye. Then I have to meet my father and sister. We're dining with the mayor and William Byers, the owner of the *Rocky Mountain News*."

Lucky Byers, Fargo thought. Then she was in his arms again, mashing her whole body against him, her soft arms around his neck. Their mouths fused and she parted her lips to admit his tongue. A groan escaped her, her arms tightening like pythons.

Fargo had to pry himself loose to say, "An

hour is plenty of time. We can take it nice and slow."

"I don't want it nice," Amity declared huskily, "and I don't want it slow." Raw passion smoldered in her eyes.

Fargo embraced her again, his hands roving over her back, down around her hips, and up to caress her breasts. Her whole body was hot to the touch, even through her dress. She was ablaze with passion, with cravings long suppressed. Her fingers clawed at his neck and shoulders, and at his buckskins as if she wanted to rip them from his body.

"I want you," she whispered in his ear.

Fargo could tell. Suddenly sweeping her into his arms, he turned and deposited her on the bed. Lying there with her red lips in a tantalizing pout, a knee slightly bent, and her whole body squirming in ardent anticipation, she set his blood to boiling. He locked the door, threw his hat onto the dresser, removed his gunbelt, and sank down beside her.

Amity clutched him as if she were drowning and he were a floating log. She ground herself against him, her legs creating enough friction to mill flour. Her mouth was everywhere; on his lips, his chin, his cheeks, his brow, his ears. She devoured him with her hands as well, her fingers exploring every square inch of his body.

Gripping her wrist, Fargo placed her right hand squarely on his hardening manhood. Amity gasped and stiffened. She closed her eyes, her throat bobbing as she timidly curled her fingers around his member.

"Oh, my. I didn't expect this."

Fargo nuzzled her neck and she squirmed deliciously. As he licked her, he unfastened some of her buttons and stays. Her hot mouth feasted on his ear, her fiery breaths sending shivers down his spine. Lower down, she grew bold and fondled him.

As her dress unfolded like the petals of a flower, Fargo lowered his lips to the top of her cleavage. His tongue traced circles on one breast, then the other. Amity had small, pert nipples which were exceptionally sensitive to his touch. When he flicked one, she bent her body like a bow and exhaled loudly.

"Yesss. I like that. Do it again."

She didn't need to urge Fargo twice. He sucked on the other nipple, his hands, meanwhile, roaming high and low. Her thighs spread wide at his touch and he slid a hand between them. She gripped his hair at his temples, her eyelids fluttering.

"Ah! Ah! No man has ever touched me there."

Shock almost caused Fargo to stop. He knew she had shunned men, but he hadn't realized she had taken it so far as to totally deprive herself of male companionship. Somehow he'd taken it for granted she must have had a few lovers, at the very least. To learn otherwise, to learn he would be her first, was both flattering and mildly unnerving.

It had been Fargo's experience that a woman's first attempt at making love influenced the whole rest of her life. If it was pleasurable, if the woman enjoyed herself, her

163

entire future outlook on making love would be a good one. If it wasn't pleasurable, a woman would shy away from ever sharing herself again. He wanted to make Amity's first time as enjoyable as he possibly could. Only having an hour, though, complicated things. He'd rather have two, or even three.

Where normally Fargo might have dallied at her breasts forever, now he had to remind himself to attend to other parts of her ripe, quivering body. He undid more of her dress, clear down to her waist. He nibbled at her ribs, nipped at her stomach. His tongue rimmed her navel.

Amity was panting. "I feel as if I'm on fire!"

Reaching down, Fargo slid her hem up her legs as high as her knees. Her calves were firm and shapely, a hint of treasures to come. He stroked them, slowly rising higher with each upward sweep of his arm until his fingers were traveling halfway up her silken inner thighs.

Tugging at his buckskin shirt, Amity loosened it so her hands could slide up underneath and caress his hard muscles. Her fingernails scraped his skin. When he lightly pinched her nipple, she brazenly did the same to him.

Fargo's right hand massaged its way higher, almost to the junction of her thighs. He felt her tense up, as if afraid of his touch. So he held off, contenting himself with rubbing her thighs and sucking on her tongue until he was sure she had relaxed again. Then, a twist of his wrist, and his hand covered her womanhood.

"Ohhhhhhh!" Amity bucked, overcome, her hips vaulting toward the ceiling. Her legs spread even wider. "Now!" she said. "Now!"

Not quite, Fargo reflected. She wasn't ready yet, despite what she might think. His forefinger gently glided along her moist folds. Amity thrashed wildly, tossing her head from side to side in abandon. Easing onto his knees, Fargo lowered his pants but resisted when she sought to pull him into her. It was still too soon.

"Please, Skye. Please!"

Fargo silenced her plea with a kiss that went on and on, their tongues dipping and swirling. Her nipples poked into his chest as his fingers kneaded the backs of her thighs. Her fingers dug into his lower back.

Amity had closed her eyes but she opened them again when Fargo began to slowly slide a finger into her molten center. Her inner walls contracted and she hunched her bottom forward to bury him deeper. His thumb brushed her pulsating core. At the contact, Amity went into a paroxysm of ecstasy, her limbs churning as she mewed uncontrollably.

"Never knew!" Amity exhaled. "I never knew!"

Fargo didn't need to ask what she was referring to. But she hadn't felt anything yet. He levered his finger in and out as his mouth fastened onto an earlobe. The combination drove her to new heights. She nearly heaved them both off the bed. Then, pulling his broad shoulders lower, she looped her ankles high up around his back.

"When?" Amity asked him. "When will it be?"

"Do you think you're ready?"

"I've never been more ready for anything in my entire life," was her frank reply.

Fargo rubbed his pole between her upturned legs. It set his body to tingling mightily and Amity to trembling. She tensed up again when he started to ease into her, so he slid back out, biding his time. He kissed her shoulders, her breasts. Her fingers cupped the base of his member, bringing a lump to his throat.

Gradually Amity's tension melted away. When next Fargo touched his manhood to her tunnel, she didn't stiffen or draw back. She welcomed him eagerly, thrusting upward, her legs wrapped tighter so he couldn't pull away. Their eyes met, hers posing a question, a hunger, a partial fear all in one, and for a second the two of them were still.

"Now," Fargo said.

Amity cried out at his first stroke. She cried out at his second. Again at his third. From then on her cries were soundless, joy imprinted in her expression, in the increasing urgency of her thrusts. She drove up against him without reservation, holding nothing back, accepting him fully.

Fargo steeled himself against a rising inner urge to let himself go, to pound into her to gain quick release. He paced himself for her benefit, delaying his explosion to add to her bliss. Cooing softly, Amity sliced her nails deep into his shoulders. Her hips matched the tempo of his rocking form. Suddenly she

166

threw her head back. Her legs became steely bands. Fargo felt her deluge, which seemed to go on forever. When she was spent she sagged, only to stare in amazement as it dawned on her it wasn't over.

The seconds became minutes, the minutes adding up until a quarter of an hour had gone by. By then they both were caked with perspiration. Amity convulsed two more times in sheer ecstasy, and soon Faro was on the brink himself. They kissed, and his right hand covered a breast. That was when his body decided it wouldn't be denied any longer.

Together, they crested on a wave of soaring passion, the bed bouncing like a bucking bronc. Afterward, they lay in one another's arms, Amity lavishing kisses on his chest and neck. Finally she sat up and announced, "I must go. My father and Delicia will be wondering where I got to."

Rising onto an elbow, Fargo watched her dress. Shyly, she turned her back to him and didn't turn around until she was done.

"Thank you," Amity said.

"Any time."

Amity unlocked the door, then gave him a searching look. "I'm sorry."

"For what?"

Not answering, Amity Cadwell hurried out, leaving Fargo with more to ponder than ever before.

11

The second expedition "to the richest diamond fields in the history of the world," as Professor Cadwell boasted of his find time and again, wasn't anything like Skye Fargo expected it to be. He figured Rupert would invite a few leading citizens and blindfold them in order to keep the exact location a secret. Instead, over fifty of Denver's most prominent, and wealthiest, individuals were allowed to come along, learning the exact location of the claim.

In addition, since Fargo couldn't possibly handle all the pack animals by himself, Rupert hired half a dozen more men to tend to them and handle camp chores. All were recommended by William Byers, who vouched for their integrity.

The journey up took a day and a half longer than last time. With so large a group, it couldn't be helped. Denver's elite treated the excursion as a lark, as a ready-made excuse to drink and socialize and generally enjoy themselves. They took their sweet time. And as eager as Rupert was to get there, he wasn't rash enough to anger potential investors by demanding they get off their lazy backsides and ride a bit faster.

Fargo was generally left to himself. He always rode slightly ahead of the rest during the day, and at night, while the Cadwells mingled with their guests, he sat by the fire, listening and observing while sipping his coffee.

Every so often Amity or Delicia spent a few minutes with Fargo. But by and large they were usually by their father's side, lending their considerable charms to his pitch for investment capital and giving their opinions of how rich the strike would turn out to be.

"This is a once in a lifetime opportunity," Rupert said a hundred times if he said it once. "Think of it, gentlemen! Diamonds! More precious than rubies, more valuable than gold and silver! It is my esteemed professional judgment that in the first year alone the yield will top a million dollars. The profits will be enormous! Like none you've ever heard of! And you can share in these riches for a paltry twenty-five thousand dollars a share! A pittance, for men like yourselves."

Reflected in many of the faces ringing the professor, Fargo noted, was pure, undisguised greed.

"But what guarantee do we have?" asked one whose face shone like a moon.

"The best guarantee in the world," Rupert answered suavely. "The testimony of your own eyes. When you've seen the diamond fields for yourself, when you've pulled diamonds from the ground with your own two hands, then you'll know beyond a shadow of a doubt that every word I have uttered is Gospel."

Another man, in a suit that cost more than the average worker earned in a year, remarked, "If everything you've told us turns out to be true, I'll invest a quarter of a million in your venture myself."

"I'll invest three hundred thousand," another declared.

Others added amounts they would contribute. Fargo didn't keep an exact tally, but he estimated the total was close to four million dollars.

Professor Cadwell smiled expansively. "Gentlemen, gentlemen! Your generosity stirs me mightily! But I urge you to exercise foresight. Don't commit yourselves until you have seen the diamond fields for yourself. The proof, as they say, will be in the pudding."

"I must say," one of Denver's wealthiest remarked, "it's refreshing to deal with someone so honest, someone more concerned about the welfare of others than he is in lining is own pockets. You are a credit to the human race."

Fargo drew a few odd looks when he inadvertently snorted. "Some coffee went down the wrong pipe," he explained, thumping his chest.

Finally the grand moment came. They arrived at the talus early in the afternoon. Fargo reminded them how dangerous it was, and how treacherous talus could be, but he wasted his breath. When Rupert invited them to spread out and search, a frantic rush ensued, everyone running every which way, or trying to. Slipping and sliding, scrambling wildly, they swarmed up over the talus like locusts gone amok.

It was a sight to behold.

The frenzy grew worse when one of Denver's upper crust lifted a rock and screeched, "I've found one! Look here! I've found one!" He waved his find for all to see, a rough diamond about as big as a strawberry.

Bedlam ensued. Dirt and stones and large rocks flew thick as hail. More diamonds were unearthed, and each fueled the craving of those who hadn't found any. Many fell. Many were bruised. Clothes were ripped and smeared with grime. But none of them cared. They scurried about like madmen, heedless of the risk, some almost breaking their necks when they took bad spills.

Fargo sat down below with the men Byers had hired to handle the pack animals. It turned out they all worked for the newspaperman in one capacity or another. Two were employed in the shipping department. Another oversaw deliveries. They told Fargo that Byers had walked into the *News* the other day, called all his employees together, and asked if any would like to earn extra wages on a little jaunt into the mountains.

"Look at them up there!" a stringbean in overalls said. "I've never seen the like in all my born days."

"They're acting like a bunch of chickens with their heads chopped off," a second worker mentioned.

"That's what too much money does to a people," a third said. "They get all loco."

"Hell, who do you think you're kidding?" a fourth declared. "Any one of us would give

171

our eyeteeth to have half the money they do. Being rich and crazy beats being poor and miserable any day of the year."

They looked at Fargo as if thinking he would have something to say on the subject but he didn't. Not yet, anyway.

Thirty-six diamonds were found. That evening flasks were passed around and the well-heeled Denver crowd celebrated. Everyone was giddy at the prospect of adding greatly to their already substantial bank accounts. Professor Cadwell was toasted again and again. They heaped praise on his shoulders for being, as William Byers remarked, "the man who has brought our fair city to new heights of glory, who will enrich our coffers beyond our wildest dreams, who will forever be enshrined in the history books. Thanks to you, Rupert, Denver will soon rival New York, Philadelphia and San Francisco."

"My blushes, gentlemen," Cadwell said. "All I am is a humble gemologist. If I reap a few financial rewards in the pursuit of my profession, so be it."

The next morning they started back down. Fully a third of the well-to-do were not very well off. They moved about as if freshly risen from the grave, moving stiffly, their features pale, flinching whenever anyone talked too loud.

William Byers wasn't one of them; he didn't approve of heavy drinking. After an hour on the trail he trotted his mount up next to the Ovaro. "You must be very proud of your part in this glorious venture."

"More or less," Fargo said.

"When we get back I'm issuing a special edition of the *News* to report the results of our search. Naturally, I'll have the diamonds examined to verify their authenticity. But that's a mere formality. I'm sure they're the genuine article."

"Are you planning to invest in the mining company?"

Byers snickered. "Need you ask? I would be a fool not to. I intend to take twenty-five thousand out of the bank and buy a share." He glanced over his shoulder to insure no one was close enough to hear. "It's all I can afford, I'm afraid. Being a newspaper owner carries more prestige than it does financial rewards."

Fargo scanned the slope below. No further attempts on his life had been made in days, but he wouldn't relax his guard. There were bound to be others. "We need to have a long talk once we reach Denver."

"About what?"

Hooves drummed. Delicia, smiling sweetly, joined them. "What are you two doing up here all by yourselves?"

"Talking about the diamonds, like everyone else," Fargo answered before the journalist could.

"My father wants to see you, Bill," Delicia told Byers. "Something about a series of advertisements he wants to run in your paper to promote the sale of shares."

Byers laughed. "As if any are needed! He already stands to be a millionaire before the week is out."

173

Delicia's face was positively angelic. "The more capital he can raise, the more equipment he can buy and the more men he can hire. He wants to get off to a running start."

"He'll do that, and more," Byers said, reining his mount around. With a wave, he galloped back.

Delicia leaned toward Fargo, placing her hand on his arm, and giving him a playful squeeze. "How are you holding up, handsome? I'm sorry I haven't been able to spend much time with you, but you can see how hectic everything is."

"I know how things are," Fargo confirmed.

"But in a few days that will change," Delicia said. "Once my father has sold all the shares, he'll be busy getting his company off the ground. I should have more time to myself." She winked. "I'll come pay you a visit."

Fargo gazed off down the mountain so she wouldn't notice the resentment he felt at her bald-faced lie. "I can't wait."

Shortly before noon, Fargo halted the caravan. He checked on the pack animals, then walked a dozen yards to a stand of aspens. Rupert was rambling on and on again about how everyone who invested would reap a bonanza, and Fargo couldn't stand to listen to it anymore. He idly plucked a blade of grass and stuck it in his mouth.

Amity strolled over. Of the three Cadwells she was the most subdued, the one who didn't prattle on endlessly about the diamonds. Without being asked she sat down close to him, hugged her knees to her bosom, and sighed. "I wish we'd had more time together."

Shades of Delicia, Fargo reflected. "In my hotel room, you mean?" he played along.

"I feel as if I have no control, as if I'm a pebble caught up in a rockslide."

Fargo chewed on the blade of grass.

"This is the way my whole life has been," Amity complained. "Our father has dragged us all over creation, chasing one rainbow after another. When I was little I didn't mind much. It was exciting. A new adventure every day." She paused. "But now I'd like to slow the pace down. To have a life of my own. I dream of having a home one day, of a husband and children." Amity looked at him. "Is that so wrong?"

"Who says it is?"

"Delicia, for one. She thinks it's silly of me. But then, she'll never settle down, not so long as she has her looks and men flock to her like children to candy."

"What's good for her might not be good for you." Fargo saw her sister over by the horses, surrounded by ardent admirers. It was plain she relished being the center of attention.

"Rupert agrees with her, though," Amity said. "He doesn't want me to dig in roots, either. He says we should stick together always."

Fargo removed the blade of grass from his mouth and flipped it to one side. "Sooner or later we all have to stand on our own two feet."

"I know. But it's easier said than done. They rely on me and on my business sense.

175

Without me, they wouldn't have gotten half as much as they have. Delicia is better at spending money than making it."

Fargo sensed that Amity wanted to say more, that she was deeply troubled. He waited, hoping she would confide in him.

"I wish we could turn back the clock," Amity presently remarked. "I wish we could go back and live our lives all over again, knowing what we know now. I'd do it all differently. I'd go off on my own and live my life on my own terms."

"Wishful thinking," Fargo said. He didn't mean it to sound cruel, but Amity flinched as if he had slapped her.

"You're right, of course. No amount of wishful fancies can change the past. What's done is done. The burden for our mistakes falls on our shoulders and ours alone." Shaking herself, Amity stood. "Sorry to go off on a tangent like that."

"Is that what it was?"

"What else would it be?" Amity sparred. Straightening her shoulders, she walked toward Delicia. "Guess I better make myself useful. Thanks for listening."

"Any time," Fargo responded. To himself, much more softly and with more than a tinge of regret, he said, "Any time at all."

The special edition of the *Rocky Mountain News* had the whole city buzzing like a stirred hive of bees. Diamonds were on everyone's lips. Groups gathered on street corners to discuss the find and what it meant for Denver.

Practically every person Fargo and Marshal Tom Hendly passed were doing the same. A total stranger stopped them to ask what they thought, and Fargo answered honestly.

"I stopped believing in fairy tales when I was six."

Fargo and the lawman arrived at the *Rocky Mountain News* offices just in time. The windows were dark, and the owner himself was locking the front door.

"Mr. Fargo! Tom!" Byers exclaimed. "This is a surprise. What brings the two of you here?"

"We need to talk, Bill," Hendly said.

"Is that so?" Byers had on a neatly pressed suit and high hat. "Can't it wait? The city fathers are holding a banquet in Professor Cadwell's honor in an hour and I'm the featured speaker. Everyone who is anyone will be there, the cream of Denver's crop. I can't be late."

Hendly took a folded sheet of paper from inside his vest. "You'd better read this. Fargo asked me to do some checking while you were up in the mountains and this is part of what I turned up."

"What sort of checking?" Byers impatiently scanned the sheet. Soon enough, his eyes narrowed, and his jaw hardened. "Tell me this is a cruel joke. There must be some mistake."

"I wish there were," Marshal Hendly said. "I know how much this meant to you. But better late than sorry. A month from now, and you'd be out the money you invested. To say nothing of all the others."

"Lord, they almost pulled it off!" Byers declared, severely upset. "I should call a meeting of the Committee of Safety and have them strung from the highest cottonwoods along Cherry Creek!"

"Since when do you hang women, Bill?" Hendly said.

William Byers was in a funk. Shaking the paper at Fargo, he demanded, "Why didn't you say something sooner? How long have you known?"

"I didn't say anything because I didn't have proof," Fargo explained. "And I wasn't completely sure until our second trip into the mountains."

Sliding a pocket watch from his jacket, Byers consulted it. "My guess is they're still at the Grand. We'll go directly there. If we miss them, we'll go on to the banquet hall. This farce must end tonight!" He stormed off.

"Hold on," Marshal Hendly said. "We have to do this by the letter of the law."

Fargo tagged along, although they didn't need him. The marshal had all the proof they required. But he wanted to be there when it all came crashing down, if only to learn whether a certain part of their bold scheme had been a lie like all the rest.

The flustered doorman at the Grand Hotel hustled aside to admit the newspaper owner and the lawman. Byers stalked by him without so much as a glance, marching straight to the stairs with Hendly glued to his footsteps.

Merry laughter confirmed the Cadwell clan was still there. All three were in Rupert's room.

He answered Byers's booming knock wearing his white suit, which had been cleaned and starched, with a warm smile of welcome. Behind him, preening at a mirror, were his daughters.

"William! To what do I owe this honor? Don't tell me you've come to personally escort us there?"

Byers grabbed Cadwell by the throat. "You fraud! You stinking, scheming, rotten fraud! You deserve to be shot like a dog for your unmitigated gall!"

Amity and Delicia rushed over, stopping midway at the sight of Marshal Hendly, who entered with his revolver drawn. Fargo came last and leaned against the jamb.

"What's going on here?" Delicia asked. "How dare you burst in here and manhandle my father!"

"Spare us the act!" Byers thundered. "We know! Damn your wretched, deceiving hides, we know what you've done!"

Fargo had to hand it to Cadwell. The professor's self-control was superb. Smiling, Cadwell put a hand on the editor's shoulder.

"Please, William, get a hold of yourself. I can't begin to guess what has you so disturbed. But whatever it is, whatever the problem might be, we can work it out."

Byers was too mad to listen to reason. He cocked a fist but Marshal Hendly gripped his arm and pulled him back.

"None of that, Bill. I'm taking them into custody. You can file a formal complaint if you want, but that's all. No violence. No vigilantes. Savvy?"

Rupert visibly tensed. "Vigilantes?"

"The Committee of Safety doesn't take kindly to swindlers and cheats," Byers said. "Usually we make the punishment fit the crime, but in your case there isn't a punishment fitting enough. Now that I think about it, even hanging is too good for you. You should spend the rest of your days rotting in prison."

Delicia brought her beauty and charm to bear. "Please, Mr. Byers! Marshal! Will someone kindly tell us what this is all about?"

The lawman did the honors. "I did some checking, lady. I went through all the wanted circulars in my file cabinet, and then I did some research down at the *News,* searching through back issues. It didn't take long to find what I was looking for."

Amity broke her silence. "Which was what, exactly?" Demurely clasping her hands, she slowly sidled toward the bed.

"Who you really are. For starters, your last name isn't Cadwell." Marshal Hendly pointed at Rupert. "You're really Alfred Durst, a swindler and cheat from Florida." The marshal nodded at Delicia. "Your name is Emily Stegall, and you hail from Georgia. And you, ma'am—" the lawman addressed Amity—"were born Cynthia Whitney in Raleigh, North Carolina. The three of you are wanted in half a dozen states on more charges than I can shake a stick at."

Rupert—or Alfred, or whatever his name truly was—adopted an indignant attitude. "There must be some mistake, my good fellow. I can show you my credentials. My degrees are in my suitcase."

"Degrees as counterfeit as you are," Marshal Hendly said. "After I got done going through the back issues of the paper, I rode out to the survey camp east of here—"

"Survey camp?" Rupert interrupted.

"The Army Corps of Topographical Engineers is doing a survey of the foothills hereabouts," the lawman said. "The man in charge, Hayden, is a geologist. I asked him about you."

"So?" Rupert refused to admit he was beaten. "I don't recall ever meeting anyone by that name. What does that prove?"

"It proves you're a fake," Hendly said. "He told me there is no such thing as a doctor of gemology. And when I showed him one of those diamonds you turned up on your first trip into the mountains, he said it came from Africa, not from the Rockies."

"He was mistaken—" Rupert began.

"Not hardly," Marshal Hendly said. "He suspects you had some diamonds brought into the country through a dealer in Holland. Then you salted the talus slopes to make it seem as if tons of them were lying there for the taking."

Delicia rallied to her fictitious father's defense. "That's absurd!"

Fargo had been watching Amity. She was only a step or two from the foot of the bed, and her traveling bag. "I saw you do it," he said. "Oh, you had me hoodwinked for a while. That day on the talus, I thought you were

181

putting diamonds into all of those leather pouches you carried. But after you feel asleep, I looked inside them. All I found was one small diamond."

"We put the rest in Rupert's saddlebags," Delicia said.

"Nice try. But you weren't *collecting* diamonds," Fargo said. "You were *planting* them for the investors to find."

Amity had reached the bedpost. She fiddled with her dress, her other hand dropping toward her bag. As she started to reach into it, Fargo palmed the Colt. "Your derringer stays where it is," he warned.

"I'd never have shot you," Amity said, her features betraying deep hurt.

Marshal Hendly grabbed the bag, fished out the derringer, and stuck it into his pocket. "The three of you are coming with me. You'll go up before the judge in a few days. He'll decide whether to put you on trial here or to ship you to one of the other states who want you."

Rupert was crestfallen. "Surely, my good man, you're not going to keep us in jail until then? I give you my solemn word we won't try to flee your jurisdiction."

The lawman chortled. "And you expect me to believe you? Mister, if lies were gold, you wouldn't need to strike it rich."

Amity hadn't taken her eyes off Fargo. "The empty leather pouches were all that gave us away?"

"No. There were other things, here and there," Fargo said. He didn't go into detail. There was no need.

Marshal Hendly gestured. "So you admit your guilt, Miss Whitney? You might as well, and make it easier on yourself."

"I admit nothing," Amity said defiantly.

William Byers had calmed down considerably. Checking his pocket watch, he announced, "I must go break the news to the city fathers. I only hope they can find it in their hearts to forgive me for being taken in by these charlatans." He glared spitefully at Rupert, then breezed on out, saying over his shoulder. "May all of you rot in hell."

"You'll regret your impertinence when you learn I was telling the truth!" Rupert hollered after him.

"Give it up," Marshal Hendly said. "Your descriptions match those on the circulars perfectly. Now let's get you to the jail so I can go to supper."

"Are we allowed to take anything?" Delicia asked.

"A hairbrush and a change of clothes, that's all."

Amity stuffed her riding outfit into her travel bag. Shouldering it, she stepped to the doorway.

Fargo asked the question that had been uppermost on his mind since his suspicion crystalized. He had to know. "Was everything you told me a lie?"

"No," Amity whispered, her lips hardly moving. "Not everything." She cleared her throat. "I never misled you about my personal life. Not once." Her fingers brushed against his. "Whatever else you might think of me, I hope you will believe that much, at least."

Rupert and Delicia filed out after her, both hanging their heads. Marshal Hendly was next. Fargo came last, closing the door and turning just as there was a sound of a hard object striking flesh and then the heavy thud of a body hitting the floor. His hand darted toward his Colt but it was already too late.

The lawman lay on his side unconscious, a nasty gash in his temple. Straddling him, holding a cocked Remington, was Ike Talbot. And behind Talbot were three more gunmen, one of them Gill, the assassin who had fled from the alley the other night. All three held leveled rifles.

12

At night, from the foothills, the lights of Denver resembled sparkling fireflies. The sounds of the city had long since faded, and other than the creak of saddle leather and the dull thud of hooves, all Skye Fargo heard was the soft weeping of Delicia Cadwell. Even though Fargo knew her real name was Emily, he still thought of her as Delicia. It fit her better.

Ike Talbot, who was just ahead of Fargo, shifted in the saddle to glare at her. "Stop that blubbering, bitch."

"You have no call to talk to her like that," Rupert said. His horse was behind Fargo's dun.

"What do you expect after the way you slapped her around?" Like Fargo, Rupert's wrists were bound. His white suit was disheveled, his bowler gone, knocked off by one of the three gunmen when he objected to being forced from the hotel at gunpoint and was struck across the temple.

"You ain't too bright, are you, fat man?" Talbot sneered. "I can do any damn thing I want. If you want to reach the diamond fields with all your teeth in your mouth, don't give me any sass."

Rupert sighed. "How many times must I tell you? There are no diamonds. It was all a swindle."

"Sure it was," Talbot said, and laughed. "Nice try. But I can read. I saw in the newspaper how you and the Trailsman took all those big-wigs up into the high country, and how they were pulling diamonds out of the ground right and left."

"Tell him, Mr. Fargo," Rupert urged. "Maybe he'll listen to you since I can't seem to get through to him."

"Nothing we say will change his mind," Fargo said. And why should it? The story in the *News* was all the proof Talbot needed. The next edition of the paper, the one detailing the professor's scheme to milk millions from Denver's gold-rich elite, wouldn't hit the streets until tomorrow. By then they would be well up into the mountains.

"Damn right it won't," Talbot crowed. "This is the lucky break I've been waiting for! I can finally get out from under Charley Harrison's shadow. The boys and me will gather up all the diamonds we can carry and light a shuck to California. We'll set ourselves up like kings. Maybe I'll open up my own saloon in San Francisco, where I'll be the cock of the walk, just like Harrison is here."

"You don't sound very fond of him," Fargo commented.

"Fond?" Talbot practically spat the word. "I despise the bastard. I hate how he lords it over us as if we're his slaves or something." Talbot shifted around again. "Why do you think I went to so much bother to pit the two of you against each other?"

Fargo wanted to smack himself for not having caught on sooner. "*You're* the one who put the bounty on my head?"

"Of course. I wanted you to think Harrison did it so you'd go gunning for him. But nothing ever came of it. I was about ready to make wolf bait of him myself when I read all about the professor here."

"But there are no diamonds!" Rupert persisted. "Dragging us up there will avail you nothing. What will it take to get that through your thick head?"

Ike Talbot wheeled his mount and brought it alongside Rupert's. "I told you to shut up," he snapped, and slapped Rupert's cheek with enough force to nearly unhorse him. "I don't want to hear any more of your lies. Remember, old man. I don't need you to find the diamond fields. Fargo knows where they are, too. I'm only keeping you alive because you can tell the really valuable ones from those the newspaper says aren't so valuable."

"What about us?" Amity asked. She was behind Rupert, Delicia, in turn, behind her. The three gunmen were at the rear to insure no one tried to escape. "Why have you brought my sister and me along?"

"Talk about stupid questions." Talbot chortled. "After we've collected enough diamonds, the boys and I plan to do some celebrating. We've brought some whiskey along, and you two ladies will provide the entertainment."

"I'd rather die," Amity said. "Shoot me now and be done with it."

Talbot ogled her and licked his lips. "Sorry. I'm not about to let anything happen to that fine body of yours until after we're done with you. Then, who knows?" Shrugging, he kneed his horse forward, slowing when he was even with the dun. "What about you, Fargo? Anything you want to say?"

"No."

"Smart hombre. Just remember. Any tricks, and I'll put a slug in you. Not to kill, mind you, just to cripple. I need you to lead us to the diamonds, but I don't need you in one piece to do it, Savvy?"

Fargo nodded. Talbot, smirking, rode on ahead. Fargo resumed straining against the rope binding his wrists, rubbing them back and forth, seeking to loosen the rope enough to free himself. It felt a little strange to be on another horse other than the Ovaro. The dun had been waiting in back of the Grand Hotel along with the rest of their mounts and two pack animals which the last gunman in line was leading.

Ike Talbot had had it all planned out, but he hadn't counted on running into Marshal Hendly, whom they had left lying in the hallway. Fargo had been worried they might murder the lawman, but Talbot surprised him. Probably because Talbot didn't want to start his new life in California a wanted man.

For hours now they had been steadily climbing. It was well past midnight and Talbot showed no indication of stopping anytime soon. Delicia was exhausted, her chin drooping. Amity had to be equally tied but she held her head high to spite her captors.

For their benefit, Fargo asked, "How much longer before we stop? The women need to rest."

"Too bad for them," Talbot said. "We're not slowing down until sunrise. We'll sleep during the day and ride at night. Less chance of being spotted that way."

It was also more dangerous. In the dark a horse could blunder into a hole or rut, or hurt itself in a variety of other ways. And at night grizzlies and mountain lions were abroad, to say nothing of rattlers, which did most of their hunting after the sun went down.

"I couldn't believe it when I saw the newspapers," Talbot was saying. "Diamonds! And we can pluck them right up! Like taking eggs from a basket, the paper says." He glanced at Fargo. "You were there. You saw it with your own eyes. Did you help yourself to one when nobody was looking?"

"No."

"What kind of idiot are you? I'd have snuck to the diamond fields in the middle of the night and stuffed my saddlebags full, then made myself scarce." Talbot chuckled. "All these years of racking my brain for a way to get rich. Who would have thought it would turn out to be so easy?"

On through the night they rode, the wind intensifying, bringing with it an unseasonable chill. Fargo, in his buckskins, was reasonably comfortable, but the two women were in dresses too thin to afford much warmth. Delicia complained until Ike Talbot growled for her to keep quiet or he would gag her, adding, "You'll be hot enough once the sun comes up. Think warm thoughts of you and me until then."

Fargo felt sorry for the women but there was nothing he could do. Talbot wouldn't listen to reason. All Amity and Delicia could do was suffer until dawn.

It was a long time coming. The hours crawled by. Fargo's eyelids were leaden when at long last a faint pink tinge heralded the advent of the new day.

Talbot veered into a wooded tract and dismounted. "We'll lie low here until sunset. Gill, you and Harve keep watch until noon, then wake Sam and me. We'll spell you until it's time to head out."

Rupert groaned as he slid off. "How about something to eat and drink? Surely you don't intend to starve us to death?"

Talbot laughed. "Mister, you could go

without food for a month of Sundays and still look like a pumpkin. You'll get some grub this evening. I'm not making a campfire until I'm sure no one is trailing us."

Fargo doubted anyone was. Marshal Hendly might have glimpsed the gunmen before being slugged, but the lawman had no idea what Talbot was up to. Hendly wouldn't know where to begin to look, and certainly wouldn't suspect Talbot was on his way to the talus slopes.

Amity climbed down and arched her spine. One of the hardcases whistled and winked but she ignored him.

As for Delicia, she was so tired she could barely stand. Shuffling toward a tree, she sank down with her back to it, then winced. "Every muscle I have is stiff and sore. And I'm cold as ice." She motioned at Ike Talbot. "Can I please have a blanket to cover myself?"

"You can cover yourself with me, sweetie," said the young gunman who had whistled.

"Hands off, Sam," Talbot said. "We agreed, remember? No fooling around until after we have the diamonds. Then you can do whatever you want."

Sam cupped his groin and made thrusting movements at Delicia. "Did you hear that, gorgeous? You think you're sore now, but when this is over I'm going to ride you into the ground."

"Is that tiny twig of yours supposed to scare me?" Delicia countered. "I've made love to *real* men."

One of the other hardcases laughed. Sam,

190

reddening, started toward her, his fists balled, his spurs jangling.

"Don't even think of it!" Ike Talbot said sternly, and Sam stopped. "No one is to harm a hair on their pretty heads! So long as we have these ladies in our power, the professor will be all too glad to pick out the best diamonds for us." He glanced at Rupert. "Isn't that right, mister?"

"They're not my daughters, you know," Rupert stupidly mentioned.

Talbot laughed harder than ever. "You never give up, do you? First you claim there aren't any diamonds even though everyone in Denver knows better. Now you have the nerve to claim your own flesh and blood aren't related to you?"

"Newspapers don't always print the truth," Rupert said.

"Do you honestly think I'm gullible enough to believe you?" Talbot asked. "How stupid do you think I am?"

"I can answer that one," Amity piped up, and pointed at the hind end of the nearest horse.

Talbot didn't like it when his men cackled. Glaring, he advanced on her as Sam had just done.

Fargo risked the killer's wrath by stepping in front of him. "Not one hair on their pretty heads, remember?"

Snarling, Talbot made as if to hit Fargo, but didn't. "You'll all get yours soon enough," he vowed, then began barking commands.

In short order the horses were stripped of

their saddles and the packs were stacked under a pine. Ike Talbot and Sam spread their bedrolls out and were soon sound asleep. Gill and Harve took up posts at opposite ends of the camp, each with a rifle.

Fargo slumped against a trunk and pulled his hat brim low over his face so no one could tell he wasn't sleeping. Inch by gradual inch he snaked his hands toward the Arkansas toothpick. They had frisked him for weapons back at the hotel but hadn't found the ankle sheath.

Delicia was on her back, a forearm over her eyes, her bosom rising and falling rhythmically. Rupert was curled up on his side, his hands between his legs, constantly tossing and muttering to himself.

Amity was on her stomach, a cheek resting on her wrist, but Fargo, peering from under his hat brim, had a sneaking suspicion she wasn't asleep. He was sure her eyes were cracked open, and she was watching the pair on guard.

Dawn presently broke in all its glory. A blazing golden crown lit the rim of the world with vivid hues of red, orange, and yellow, and the wild creatures came alive in the surrounding forest. Birds roused from their roosts and nests trilled an avian chorus. Squirrels greeted the new day by climbing high into the branches and chattering. Chipmunks scurried madly about gathering food.

Fargo slid lower down the tree trunk and bent his knees so his hands were close to the top of his right boot. He was sliding his fingers underneath when the crunch of footsteps warned him someone was approaching.

It was grimy, greasy Gill, the one with the nervous twitch. The gunman paused, stared balefully at him, then walked over to the provisions. Rummaging in a pack, Gill pulled out a handful of jerky. Most went into his pocket. Chewing on a piece, he walked over to Harve and offered him some. They talked in low tones.

Fargo's fingers touched the top of the Arkansas toothpick's slender hilt, and he smiled inwardly as his hand closed around it. But as he began to pull it out, a slight noise drew his gaze to Amity. She was in a crouch, her eyes on the two curly wolves as she slowly moved toward the horse string.

Fargo wondered what she hoped to accomplish. He couldn't see her running off. She wasn't the kind to desert Delicia and Rupert. Then he saw the butt of a rifle jutting from the scabbard of one of the saddles placed near the string. She was going for the gun.

A glance at Ike Talbot and Sam showed Fargo they were still asleep, Talbot with a blanket pulled to his chest, young Sam buried in his. The only ones Amity had to worry about were Gill and Harve, and they had their backs to the horses. Amity just might make it. She only had about five yards to cover.

Unexpectedly, an animal nickered lightly. Amity froze, but neither of the sleeping killers stirred, nor did the gunmen standing guard look around. She moved on, avoiding dead twigs and dry leaves. When Sam rolled onto his back, she stopped, fear of discovery etched in her features. But the young hardcase didn't open his eyes. Amity crept forward. Another couple of feet would do it.

"Just what do you reckon you're doing, missy?" Ike Talbot sat up, his Remington in his hand. Amity pivoted and turned to stone. "Gill! Harve!" he roared. "Quit jawing like biddy hens and get the hell over here!"

The two cutthroats came on the run. Gill, swearing like a river rat, seized Amity by the arm and roughly flung her to the earth. "Damn you, woman!" he fumed, his twitch worse than ever. "What are you tryin' to do? Make Harve and me look like fools?"

"That's not hard to do, is it?" Talbot said angrily as he holstered the Remington. "Tie her legs. And this time, try to keep an eye on her. If she causes any more trouble, I'm holding the two of you to blame."

Gill and Harve obeyed, and none too gently, either. Amity tried to resist but she was helpless against their combined strength and was rudely dumped well away from the horses. "This will teach you," Gill said, giving her a kick in the ribs to stress his point.

Neither Rupert nor Delicia had woken up, they were so exhausted. Fargo lifted his head but then pretended to go right back to sleep. He lay motionless for over an hour, peeking under his brim now and again at the two keeping watch.

Gill had gone back to the other side of the clearing and was leaning against an oak. Harve, who was a short gun shark in a brown hat and cowhide vest, had rolled himself a cigarette and was sitting on a log to enjoy a smoke.

Fargo began to slide the toothpick out. The hilt was exposed, when all of a sudden Gill let out with a yell and barreled toward him. Fargo tensed, thinking Gill had seen what he was up to, but instead the hardcase ran to Talbot, who had risen on an elbow and was glancing around in confusion. So was Sam.

"What the hell is going on?" Ike demanded. "What was that shout?"

"A dust cloud," Gill reported, pointing to the east. "About a mile off, I figure. But whoever it is, they're following us."

Harve had dashed over at the outcry. "A posse, you reckon?"

Talbot got up, as riled as a wet hornet. "How can it be? We stuck to back streets when we rode out of Denver. No one paid any attention to us, and it was too dark for anyone to see our faces even if they had."

Gill was insistent. "It's a dust cloud, I tell you! Riders are after us. I can't tell how many but it has to be plenty."

"I hope to hell you're wrong."

The four killers hurried toward the tree line. Fargo saw that both Rupert and Delicia were now awake. He pulled the Arkansas toothpick the rest of the way out and reversed his grip, then applied the razor edge to the rope. Talbot and the gunnies were staring off down the slope, gesturing excitedly. Fargo had to cut fast. He sawed the knife back and forth, working furiously.

195

"Look out!" Amity whispered. "They're coming back!"

Fargo was only halfway through the rope. He pressed the knife between his wrists to conceal it just as Ike Talbot and the others hastened into the clearing.

Talbot was swearing a mean streak and glaring at anyone and everyone as if looking for any excuse to shoot one of them. "I can't believe our luck! It has to be that damn marshal! But how he picked up our trail, I'll never know."

"What do we do?" Gill anxiously asked. "Kidnapping a woman is a hanging offense. The circuit judge will sentence us to swing."

"You jackass," Talbot said. "Do you really think we'll live long enough to see the inside of a courtroom? The vigilantes will have us dancing a strangulation jig long before them." He stooped to gather his blanket. "Saddle up, boys? Let's burn the breeze."

Harve gestured. "What about the women and these other two? They'll only slow us down. Should we kill them?"

"And give up any hope of getting our hands on some diamonds?" Talbot rejoined. "Are you loco?"

Gill and Sam seized Fargo and half carried, half dragged him to the dun. They threw on a saddle, then dumped him on, jostling his arms so severely he nearly dropped the Arkansas toothpick. He was worried they would spot the knife but they were in too great a hurry to get out of there to pay much attention to him.

Amity was last to be put on a horse. They had to cut her ankles loose, and as she was being boosted up, Gill gave her a swat on the backside.

"Nice and soft, the way I like 'em. I'm glad we're taking you along, lady."

"Go to hell."

The four killers forked leather as Ike Talbot assumed the lead. They rode westward, up an incline that brought them to a bench below a high bluff. Skirting to the north, they had an unobstructed view of the country below, clear down to the prairie. The dust cloud, Fargo estimated, was half a mile off.

"If we get the chance we'll ambush the bastards," Talbot said.

Fargo sliced at the rope but it was slow going. The dun's rolling gait hindered him. All it would take was one slip and he'd cut his own wrists. As it was, he pricked himself twice, drawing drops of blood.

Talbot headed higher, climbing an open slope toward a serrated ridge. "From up there we can hold off a small army," he remarked.

Only a few strands were left. Fargo exerted more pressure and the rope fell off. He attempted to catch it but it slid down over his legs. Keeping his wrists close together as if they were still bound, he spurred his horse into a brisk walk to overtake Talbot. A slash to the throat was all it would take. Then he would grab Talbot's rifle and pistol and confront Gill and the others. But events decreed otherwise.

"Ike! Ike! I can see 'em now!" Harve came pounding up, waving his rifle.

Stick figures appeared over the rise, over a dozen men on horseback riding hell-bent for leather. Even at that distance the glint of tin on the chest of the foremost riders was unmistakable.

"What did I tell you?" Talbot said. "Marshal Hendly!"

"Who cares? That shiny badge of his will make a nice target," Harve replied.

Harve stayed by Talbot's side. It took ten minutes to reach the ridge, and once there the two killers hopped down and worked the levers of their rifles.

Reining up, Fargo turned his mount so it faced them. He hunched over the saddle horn as if he were tired, so neither would notice his hands were loose.

Amity, Delicia, and Rupert rode past Fargo and halted. Gill and Sam joined Ike Talbot and Harve at the rim. Catching Amity's eye, Fargo parted his forearms so she would know he was ready to make his move.

"Climb down, all of you," Talbot ordered.

Everyone did, everyone except Fargo.

"Wait until we can see the sweat on their brows, boys," Talbot told the other gunmen. "Pick off the lawman first. The rest might turn tail."

Fargo pulled his right boot from the stirrup as if he were preparing to climb down but instead he suddenly lashed the reins and rammed his heels into the dun's sides. The horse bounded forward—right at the gunmen. Sam and Harve were violently bowled over. Gill brought up his Spencer but Fargo planted his boot in the hardcase's face and sent him staggering. That left Ike Talbot, who sprang aside to avoid the dun and raised his own rifle.

Springing from the saddle, Fargo slammed into Talbot's chest. They both went down, tumbling to the edge. Talbot pushed to his knees and clawed at his Remington but Fargo rammed his shoulder into Talbot's midsection. Grappling, they rolled off and down the slope, gaining speed rapidly.

Fargo heard Gill yell as they went over. He concentrated on Talbot, who almost had the Remington out, and clamped his hand on the killer's wrist. Not two seconds later they crashed to a bone-jarring stop against a small boulder.

Ike Talbot was a study in fury. He tugged with all his might, seeking to break Fargo's grasp. Unable to, he grew more incensed, and drove a punch at Fargo's chin, narrowly missing when Fargo jerked his head to one side.

Above them more yells told Fargo the other gunmen were rushing to Talbot's aid. He twisted, spearing the Arkansas toothpick up and in. The slim blade pierced Talbot just below the ribs, shearing upward. Howling like a stricken wolf, Talbot threw himself backward. Blood gushed, the crimson stain spreading rapidly across his shirt.

Fargo yanked the knife out and buried it in again. There was a brief resistance as steel snagged on bone, then the toothpick lanced in to the hilt. Talbot's eyes widened. Like a punctured balloon he deflated and flopped onto his stomach.

A shot rang out, then another. Miniature

dirt geysers erupted. Diving, Fargo snatched up the Remington and swiveled onto his back. Gill, Harve, and Sam were charging him, snapping off shots as fast as they could. Fargo didn't have time to aim. He simply pointed the Remington and fired twice.

The slugs cored Harve's forehead but momentum carried him several more years. In falling, he stumbled against Gill and they went down in a tangle. Sam, however, never slowed. Sighting along his rifle, he squeezed off a shot at the self-same instant Fargo did. A breath of wind fanned Fargo's ear. Sam, arms outflung, smashed facefirst into the soil.

Fargo started to sit up. Another blast echoed off the slope. Another shot missed him by a fraction of an inch. Gill was on his knees, taking deliberate aim. Fargo thumbed back the hammer but it fell with a dry click. Either it was a misfire or the chamber in the cylinder was empty. Gill now had him dead to rights. He saw Gill grin and braced for the searing impact.

A shot boomed but nothing happened. Fargo looked down at himself, then at Gill, who was puzzled, too, clutching at a gaping hole in his throat. As Gill collapsed, Fargo glanced up at the rim, seeing Talbot's smoking rifle in the hands of Amity Cadwell. Or Cynthia Whitney. Or whoever she was.

Twenty-five minutes later Marshal Tom Hendly and fourteen deputized citizens arrived in a cloud of swirling dust. Hendly stared at the bodies and nodded. "I knew it was Talbot. I didn't get a good look at him when he slugged me, but I knew it was him."

Fargo was seated on the grassy rim, most of the weapons belonging to the gunmen beside him. "Thanks for coming after us."

"You can thank Charley Harrison. I went to the Criterion looking for Talbot and Harrison told me one of his men had overheard Talbot say something about going after the diamonds." The lawman scanned the area. "Where is that fake professor and his so-called daughters? I know Talbot brought them along."

Fargo stood. A rise to the south prevented the marshal from answering his own question. "Beats me." As deputies climbed down to gather up the hardware and attend to the dead, he climbed on the dun.

"What are you trying to pull? You must know where they are."

"I lost sight of them," Fargo said. "They could be anywhere." It would take a skilled tracker to tell which direction they had gone, thanks to an old Apache trick. He had cut a couple of blankets into strips and tied the strips over the hooves of their mounts and the pack-horses. Fargo flicked his reins. "Look me up when you get to Denver. We'll have a drink to their health."

"I hope to hell you know what you're doing," Marshal Hendly said.

Repaying a debt, Fargo almost said. Three lives for his. Or was there more to it? Did the answer lie in the wistful, sad eyes of a raven-haired beauty?

Fargo would never tell.

W